I0763611

A
Christmas
SONG

BY TURK PIPKIN

Softshoe Publishing
2600 N. Cuernavaca
Austin, Texas 78733
Book Design by David Kampa and Kelley Toombs
ISBN: 978-1-881484-11-0
Library of Congress Catalog Number: 2018911671

Pretty Paper

by Willie Nelson

CHRISTMAS IS ENDOWED WITH A MUSICAL MAGIC all its own. In Texas, that may be a posada processional, a choir at a Christmas Mass or a gospel quartet singing *Away in a Manger.* I've written Christmas songs like *Pretty Paper*—one of my favorites—and recorded several albums of Yuletide carols. Through the music of Christmas, we are all lifted higher.

I have a long and deep affection for Christmas, from childhood celebrations with my grandparents in Abbott, Texas to playing Santa for my own kids, for Christmas is a tradition that holds families together through the years and across generations.

That was the spirit of the movie *Angels Sing,* with me playing the role of Nick, a jolly old soul who may (or may not) be the real St. Nick.

Now we have *A Christmas Song,* Turk's sequel to that book and movie, which brings the story forward to a time when many people are no longer near family or the traditions they came to know as a child. Many are alone at Christmas and far too many spend Christmas without a home at all.

When I was a boy, I used to see a man with no legs who sat on the street outside of Leonard's Department Store in Fort Worth. He was selling pencils and stationery for writing Christmas cards to those you loved. In a lovely voice, he sang out a description of his wares. I later wrote a song about him called "Pretty Paper."

Pretty paper, pretty ribbons of blue
Wrap your presents to your darling from you
Pretty pencils to write I love you
Pretty paper, pretty ribbons of blue

Like my song, I hope Turk's new book will remind you that we are all destined for sharing and caring, destined to know love and to give love, no matter the circumstances. By giving, we get the true meaning and joy of Christmas.

So Merry Christmas y'all!

BOOK ONE

THE TWELVE DAYS *of* CHRISTMAS

What's to-day, my fine fellow?" said Scrooge.
"To-day!" replied the boy. "Why, Christmas Day."
"It's Christmas Day!" said Scrooge to himself.
"I haven't missed it."

—A Christmas Carol
Charles Dickens

1

'Zat You, Santa Claus?

LET'S GET ONE THING STRAIGHT. IT WAS NICK'S IDEA to sell me the house. I was passing by when I saw him putting up a 'For Sale By Owner' sign. Though I knew we couldn't afford such a grand old mansion, I felt I had to look because my family was in a tight spot. The little house we were renting had sold, and we'd been unable to find a house that fit both our budget and our family of four.

He was an older man with a white beard, wavy white hair and a twinkle in his eye. When he told me his name was Nick, I thought he might be putting me on. After a quick tour and a short parlay, the price we hit upon was way too low, and I wasn't sure if he was a con man or if he had just looked in my eyes and seen how very much I wanted to buy his house.

The actual price seemed less important to him than my agreeing to meet his verbal conditions, "an understanding between gentlemen," which required me to care for the house and to keep up the standards of the neighborhood. The yard, the trees, the paint and the gutters—it all had to be done right. I was even supposed to clean the chimney, which sounded funny coming from a white-haired guy named Nick.

I wanted to consult with my wife, of course, but Nick said there was no time. It was a "take it or leave it deal," requiring each of us to make a giant leap of faith. And so we took that leap, with Nick selling me his grand home for what I could afford to pay. You'd have to admit, that's a better gift than a partridge in a pear tree.

Because of his name and his appearance, my family came to think of him as St. Nick, a Santa Claus who walked among us, and who, after leaving his Christmas gift, chimney and all, vanished into the air like St. Nick before returning to the North Pole.

It wasn't till we moved in and neighbors began welcoming us with gifts of Christmas lights that we discovered that "neighborhood standards" meant putting up thousands of lights each December for the kind of display that I thought was the tacky side of Christmas.

Before meeting Nick, there was little love between me and the holiday season. The death of my older brother when I was a boy had left me dreading the very approach of December. My bah-humbug attitude included gripes about the commercialization of spiritual traditions and a reluctance to celebrate with my family, but these were seasonal maladies—a 12-Days-of-Christmas Syndrome not uncommon among people who've lost loved ones during the most joyful time of the year.

There's a clinical term for those who get depressed at Christmas—Seasonal Affective Disorder or SAD. Fortunately, my sadness really was temporary. By New Year's Day, I'd be good as new, so the primary problem was that I did a poor job of hiding my Grinchiness from my wife and from our kids, who loved the holiday and wanted me to join in.

Complicating matters, we lost another family member that first Christmas in our new home. My father, who everyone knew as The Colonel, died in a car accident. A hero to the end, he shielded my son, David, from harm in that accident, and to this day I wonder if I can ever live up to The Colonel's legacy.

Nick's gift of our new home helped to heal our family in that time of need and helped us renew the tradition of Walker family Christmas celebrations. Nick's gift also inspired me to write my Christmas story as a simple fable, with a few names changed—but not Nick's, of course, for you can't make up anything better than a white-haired Christmas angel named Nick.

As my book found more and more readers, people I'd never met sought me out to say how my tale had affected them, many relating how I had helped them come to grips with their own Christmas sadness.

A beautiful home, a stronger family and connections to others were frequent reminders that I owed much to Nick. Even so, there was no way to repay that debt, for since the day Nick sold us the house, I'd never seen him again.

That was ten years ago, ten years of holiday celebrations, never forgetting each year to raise a toast with our neighbors to good old Nick. We'd actually met him, neighbors and friends who had been knitted together by cheer. We believed in the Christmas miracles of our neighborhood, which deepened the faith of many of us in the original Christmas miracle.

Sometimes I envisioned Nick repeating our gift for other families in need, and pictured the joy he must feel to do so much for so many. But other than restoring a lost man's love of the holiday, I didn't know anything about him—where he'd come from, how he'd spent his life or where he'd gone after selling his home.

Now I realize the truth—that I didn't want to know. I had my miracle. And never once had I thought about the cost.

2

Carol of the Bells

AND SO I BEGIN ANOTHER TALE. TEN YEARS AFTER I last saw Nick, almost in the same spot where I'd watched him hammer in that For Sale sign, I stood at my mailbox and glanced through several Christmas cards. Among the professionally photographed family postcards and the generic Hallmark greeting cards, there was one letter that stood out—a beautiful envelope that was addressed to my first name only, Michael, on a street called Wonderland Avenue.

I marveled that the letter had found us because Wonderland Avenue is only the name of our street during our annual holiday celebration. The rest of the year our street goes by its official name, Live Oak Lane. But everyone's heard of Wonderland Avenue, I reasoned, and the mailman knows where I live.

It was impossible to overlook the envelope, which had a double border of one-penny Christmas stamps all the way around it. I counted them, 50 in all, adding up to the current rate of first-class postage. In multiple postmarks, the stamps were marked from "The North Pole," an actual postmark offered by the official North Pole U.S. Postal Office, which is located in Anchorage, Alaska.

I turned it over and looked at the back flap where the return address said only, "The West Pole."

What the heck is the West Pole? I wondered as I opened the envelope and removed a beautiful handmade card. The front of the card had a drawing of the earth with the North and South poles both marked. Near the equator on the left side of the earth was another pole sticking out from the surface with a sign that said "Merry Christmas from the West Pole!"

Then came the kicker—the card was signed at the bottom with four important letters, "Nick."

Still standing at my mailbox, I glanced around to see if someone was playing a joke on me. It had been so long since I'd seen Nick that I didn't want to accept the obvious. The man who rebuilt this old house and my love of Christmas had finally checked in again. I didn't know where he was, but I knew he was alive.

But why was he sending me a card now? And what is the West Pole? We all know the North and the South poles are the geographic points marking the axis around which the earth rotates. A third pole might make the whole world spin hopelessly out of control.

So I went inside and did a little research, and was surprised to find that the internet has thousands of references to a West Pole. Those include a popular song titled *The West Pole* by a band called The Gathering, and a Texas Independence Day gathering at a place called The West Pole.

And then I found something called The West Pole Light Show. Located just an hour away from my home, the connection seemed too great to be a coincidence. That had to be it! I'd found Nick, or I guess he'd found me, as it seemed that he'd sent me an invitation to come visit.

In addition to possibly finding Nick, the idea of seeing another neighborhood Christmas celebration had its own appeal, for the magic of Wonderland Avenue had begun to fade. Ever-larger throngs visit our famous Christmas street, often trampling flowerbeds and knocking over mailboxes in the process. When your kids start each day of the school holiday picking up empty beer cans, it doesn't exactly feel like the true spirit of Christmas.

Tired of the crowds, some of our neighbors have given up on their Christmas lights, but our house still shines bright. After all, I made a promise to Nick.

WHAT I FOUND AT THE WEST POLE LIGHT SHOW was nothing like Live Oak Lane's winter wonderland that stretches up and down several blocks of brightly lit homes and yards. By contrast, the West Pole was a single home with little more than a giant Christmas tree made of lights strung from a tall pole topped by a "West Pole" flag. There were some

Christmas displays—a manger scene and Santa's sleigh and reindeer—but they weren't even illuminated. The ordinary nature of the display had not deterred a sizable crowd from filling the sidewalk and spilling out onto the street.

I must have had a puzzled look on my face, because a young mom with two kids turned to me and said, "Don't worry—you didn't miss it."

Almost on cue, hidden speakers began to blast the Manheim Steamroller version of *Carol of the Bells*. A cheer rose from the crowd as a pyramid of lights strung from the top of the pole began flashing in time to the soaring Christmas music. My own Christmas display might best be described as "a lot of lights" and I'd never considered animating them or adding music. Our old-fashioned neighborhood celebration encourages caroling from door to door, and over the years our carolers had progressed from heart-lifting to actual wassailing—the alcohol and full voice being as important as three-part harmonies or singing on key.

There was no singing at the West Pole but there was plenty of ooh-ing and aah-ing as the LED lights on the pole began flashing up and down, racing in circles and spiraling in helixes that must have required some complex computer programming. Soon the other displays joined in with their own lights, flashing Christmas scenes that included a flying Santa and reindeer.

The music and lights rose and fell in waves until a brilliant climax of light and sound, followed by a cheer from the crowd. Then after a moment, the crowd began a low chant of, "Jerry. Jerry. Jerry."

With the bright lights fading, a second song began, the March of the Toys from Tchaikovsky's Nutcracker Suite. On cue, a tall, slender guy in a red-and-white candy-striped suit stepped off the porch and into the yard. Doffing his hat, which was adorned with giant letters spelling out "The Peppermint Man," Jerry bowed to the crowd then gestured to a tall oak tree, pointing to one high branch after another, each of them lighting in turn to show a series of big toys hanging in the branches. These appeared to be actual antiques—a tricycle, a sled, a big toy fire truck—all lighting as memories of Christmases past. As we watched in silence, a small flurry of artificial snow began to fly down around us, and as each toy on the tree was lit, the snow came harder, culminating in a blizzard as the crowd raised their hands and danced in delight.

When the music ended, a final cheer went up from the onlookers. Laughter rang out and hugs were exchanged, fake snow was shaken from their hair and jackets, then the onlookers headed back to their cars. They came; they watched, they applauded and left.

Except for me. The show had been fine, but where was Nick?

The last cars were driving away when The Peppermint Man noticed me still standing in his front yard.

"Like the show?" he asked.

"Never seen anything like it," I said, sounding more sarcastic than I'd intended. He shrugged off my tone then turned to his house, but I called after him.

"Mind if I ask you a question?"

"Got a feeling you're going to whether I mind or not," Jerry said as he turned to face me.

"Did a guy named Nick sell you this house?"

"Nick?"

"Older guy—long white hair and a beard."

"You mean St. Nick?" he answered, sounding every bit as sarcastic as he intended.

"Did he?"

This brought him back down the sidewalk to me. I gathered he'd had a fair share of weird interactions with his light show visitors, so perhaps my question wasn't as strange as it sounded.

"Listen," he said softly. "I don't know what your deal is, but my brother gave me this house, left it to me after he died."

"I'm sorry."

"It's a story. Let's go sit on the porch."

As we went up the steps, he asked me what I liked most about the show.

"The toys in the tree," I told him. "How'd you do

that anyway? I've strung a lot of Christmas lights and I'm pretty good at hiding the cords but I couldn't see any. Are there batteries up there?"

"Nope. No batteries," he said as we sat on a big porch swing. "Alan put those up there. He was my big brother; never married and no kids but he collected those old toys, including this suit I'm wearing, from a TV show we loved when we were young. When Alan had too many old toys for the garage, he started hanging them in the tree."

"What happened to him?"

"He was a smoker—finally gave up the Camels for the Lights, but it didn't save him. When they diagnosed him and said it was too late for treatment, he told me not to sweat it; said he'd be happy to see one more Christmas at home. He loved Christmas; putting those toys in the tree was his way of giving a little Christmas magic to kids in the neighborhood."

"After he died, his lawyer called me and said he'd left the house to me. My wife and kids and I had been renting a mobile home, five of us, and his gift changed everything for us. The West Pole light show is in his honor. I like to think he can look down at Christmas and see the lights."

While we talked, Jerry's wife Angie brought us some eggnog and a little bit of whiskey to put in it. We sipped our nog and I told him about my brother who died on Christmas Day and about the lights at our house, which I liked to imagine my father and brother could see from heaven.

"Good for you," Jerry told me. "So you want to see the magic tree?"

We moved under the giant spreading branches, stopped close to the trunk and looked up to the toys high above us.

"My brother planted this tree forty years ago," Jerry told me. And he ran every electric wire tight up the trunk when it was half this size. See any wires?"

I looked all around at the trunk and shook my head.

"They're inside it. He nurtured this tree; it grew fast and the trunk grew over the wires. You can see 'em down by the roots, and they come out at the top. They didn't hurt the tree cause they went straight up it. So now it's a magic Christmas tree."

"That's amazing,"I told him. "I thought I put a lot of work into my Christmas display, but I'm beginning to feel like a piker."

"There's no right or wrong," Jerry told me. "If you put up one string of lights and it makes one kid happy, what's wrong with that? Kids got enough to worry about in this world already. You think they don't hear the news about all the crazy stuff that happens, about wars and refugees and everything else? I figure kids deserve a little magic at Christmas so they can enjoy the best time of life."

"I like that," I told him.

"You know what else?" he asked as we walked to

his Christmas manger so he could prop up one of the wise men. Mary and Joseph were refugees, too, in a strange land where no one would take them in. But one innkeeper made all the difference. My wife says I'm an innkeeper-in-training. You never know when you'll be called to open your door or your heart to someone in need. If that day comes for my wife and me, we want to be ready."

Raising his eggnog, Jerry clinked his cup against mine, a toast to Christmas.

"Speaking of being ready, I've got another show to do."

We shook hands in a long moment of new friendship, then I turned for my car and home. I hadn't found Nick, but I was glad I'd come. I was about to drive away when Jerry flagged me down.

"There is one thing that's always been a mystery," he told me through my car window. "I was a little lost after my brother died. We moved into his house, and I missed him so much, especially as Christmas drew near. The only Christmas decorations he'd ever put up were the toys in that oak tree, and I'd never put up lights in my life. Then one day I came home from work and there were two big boxes sitting on my porch."

"Boxes of lights?"

"I didn't know where they came from, but there they were, so I started putting them on the house. The rest grew from there."

"Sounds like Nick," I told him. "Maybe we have more in common than we realize."

"Don't we all?" Jerry said. "Now if you don't mind, Christmas is calling."

3

A Christmas Song

HERE'S WHAT RAN THROUGH MY HEAD ON THE drive home. I have a wonderful family. We live in a beautiful home on a street with neighbors who mostly get along. My kids are healthy and my wife and I have work that we love. It's the bonus round of the American dream. I hesitate to jinx it, but in a world where so many struggle, it feels like we are blessed. And yet, there's something wrong—something missing, a hole in the middle of my good fortune. And now I know exactly what that missing something is. It's a gift unacknowledged; a debt unpaid.

It was late when I got home. In contrast to the West Pole where a crowd had been building for the second show, our street was mostly deserted, just a few cars and scattered strollers who hadn't gotten word that the light display had been cut back to weekend nights because the crowds had grown too large and so had our electric bills.

Each year after David and I finished installing our lights, our family gathers at dusk for the ceremonial throwing of the switch. In an instant, several thousand lights flash on all at once—a short-lived thrill that's followed by the kids rushing to the back of our house to check the electric meter, the hands of its dial spinning wildly as the lights out front drain our bank account out back.

An environmentalist from an early age, Molly has begun to protest our power consumption.

"Climate change is real," she says, "and we're part of the problem, not part of the solution."

Cutting the neighborhood display to three nights a week halved our December power bill, and every year David and I replace more of the old lights with new low-power LEDs. That hasn't completely mollified Molly, but it's a start.

Some of my neighbors still complain about their electric bills, but don't want to switch to more efficient lights. I'm not sure what it is about the basic human condition, but sometimes it seems more satisfying to complain than to change.

Though I'd hurried home, I'd missed family dinner—the best chance in our busy household to hear about everyone's day. Susan had introduced this tradition from her own childhood, and while it sounds like an obvious plan for any family, we knew if we didn't do it regularly and agree on rules about everyone contributing, we'd miss out on a lot of our kids' lives.

How else would you know that all the "hot" high school girls think your son is a nerd, that the 8th grade math teacher "sucks," and that a pre-schooler nearly died from taking a bite of your youngest daughter's peanut butter sandwich?

Dinner can be reheated, but not a missed conversation. Skipping the leftovers on the kitchen counter, I went upstairs to find Susan asking why little Mattie's hair was dry even though she claimed she'd showered. Staying out of that debate, I checked on Molly who yelled, "Don't come in! I'm working on Christmas presents."

At the end of the hall, David's door was open, and he sat at his desk sorting stacks of papers as more came out of his printer.

"You look busy," I said.

"Buried," David told me without looking up. "How was the West Pole? You find Nick?"

"No Nick. The show had a lot of flashy lights tied to music. The crowd loved it, but Nick was a traditional Christmas guy—I don't think he'd want me to go all Midwest disco on his beautiful house."

"*Your* beautiful house, Dad," David reminded me.

"*Our* beautiful house. So what are you working on?"

"More college applications. Early acceptance notices from Harvard were scheduled for this week and I didn't get one."

"Not yet, but there's still time."

"Maybe, but if I don't get early acceptance, my chances of a full ride are lower."

"We can borrow the money."

"We could, but I have two sisters who need to go to college, too. And if I graduate with a big debt, I'll have to take a job instead of going to medical school."

"Harvard degree followed by a job is a pretty good option."

"Dad, I may not get into Harvard so I'm applying to other schools."

"Can I help?"

"Thanks. You've done your part. It's up to me now."

After I closed the door, I stood in the hall and wondered how he'd gotten so smart and we'd gotten so lucky. Great things had happened in the years since that first Christmas in the house when we almost lost David. We'd been blessed by our baby girl, Mattie. And her big sister Molly, the little girl who had truly believed in Santa, had since grown into an accomplished pianist.

Right on cue, the opening chords of *A Christmas Song* rose from the music room downstairs. Playing beautifully, Molly was adding improvisational flourishes to the Mel Tormé sheet music she was reading while keeping perfect time. I'd played piano as a kid with my Gramma Claire constantly reminding me that the beat is the key element. "Spare the note and spoil the meter," she used to say. But somehow, I could never play through a wrong note. By striving for perfection, I doomed myself to failure.

I listened to Molly play a couple of Vince Guaraldi songs from *A Charlie Brown Christmas*, then returned to little Mattie's room to say goodnight. Susan and I had thought that two kids were blessing enough, but after a few years in this big house, we started thinking otherwise. Mattie was born on a late September morning, and we're pretty sure she was conceived soon after midnight on a beautiful Christmas Eve, one more reason to love the holiday.

"Did you find Santa Nick?" Mattie asked.

The story of Santa and our potential connection to him was practically an obsession for Mattie. Most youngsters get excited about the prospect of free Santa stuff, but how many think he gave them a house?

"I didn't find him," I confessed. "But I'm still looking."

"When you find him," Mattie said, "tell him I want a real live reindeer for Christmas."

I laughed and pointed out that we couldn't keep a reindeer.

"We don't have to keep him," Mattie concluded. "I just want to see him. Santa Nick too."

So there you have it—the ten-year transformation from a father who dreaded Christmas to the luckiest man alive. That may sound like hyperbole, but if you're getting a goodnight kiss from a little girl conceived on Christmas Day, you'd be a fool not to count your blessings.

4

O Tannenbaum

BY THIS POINT, IT MUST BE OBVIOUS THAT CHRISTMAS has become my jam, as Molly would say in her never-ending array of teen speak. Her holiday jam, on the other hand, is the Christmas piano recital, an annual conquest which started with her playing an improvisational chopsticks at age 6, and which then progressed from *O Tannenbaum* to Bartok's *Three Kings* and *Dance of the Sugar Plum Fairy*—all of them performed pretty much flawlessly.

For the first time, she was joining older and more experienced pianists for a Holiday concert at UT's Bates Recital Hall, a gorgeous room where I witnessed this modest-size girl sit down at a gigantic Steinway concert grand and silence a hall full of parents with a breathtaking performance of Chopin's *Christmas Nocturne*.

As her hands flew up and down the keys, I marveled at the music, while remembering that her skill had begun with another gift. When Nick first showed me the house, perhaps he'd seen me admiring his beautiful Baldwin grand piano, or perhaps it was simply too big to move. Either way, the end result was Nick leaving a gift note on the piano when he moved out.

Molly also had the luck of lessons from Aunt Linda, who'd learned to play from our mother Claire, another connection between generations of our family.

As Molly played, I glanced around the audience at the other parents, who I imagined were thinking their child could never follow this performance. Then out of the corner of my eye, I saw an older man in the back who, for one brief moment, I thought was Nick. That's the way it's been for me every Christmas since we bought the house, me imagining I've seen Nick among the crowd on the street, at David's basketball game, or at Molly's recital. It never turns out to be Nick, of course, despite what my heart wants me to believe.

Focused again on the music and the coming last measures, which I knew were the most difficult part, I could barely breathe as Molly brought the piece home with a perfect three-point landing.

The applause was immediate and loud, and as I glanced around with satisfaction, I noticed that the old man I'd mistaken for Nick was gone.

Later that night when Susan and I were getting ready for bed, I mentioned seeing the guy who looked like Nick.

"So you saw Nick again?" she asked, sitting down at my side. "Like last month, and last year?"

Her tone was classic Susan, partially-rooted in her work as a psychologist and therapist, but not missing a chance to make light of my obsession with Nick.

"I've got an idea," she said brightly. "Tomorrow night at the Solstice fire, how about you let go of some of that angst about Nick?"

The Solstice Fire is Susan's holiday jam. All five us fill paper bags with sand and candles for traditional *luminarias* to light a giant circle in the back yard, and we invite friends and family to a small—or not so small—bonfire and ceremony. In this circle of love, we mark the shortest day of the year and celebrate the return of the sun.

For Susan—who believes there is an answer for every problem—this bonfire is a perfect opportunity to toss something symbolic into the fire as a way of ridding yourself of anything troubling or painful from the previous year.

The year after my dad died, we held our first Solstice fire and I tossed in a dozen symbolic regrets and sorrows. Much to my surprise, these simple acts really were a relief for me. Over the years, my sister Linda has tossed many regrets into the fire, proclaiming each time that she is done with missing yet another ex-husband. Despite the marriages that didn't work, she never seems to quit smiling and always looks forward to finding new love.

In the hours since Susan's suggestion, I decided her idea that I quit obsessing about Nick was a good one. After lighting the Solstice fire, Susan generally gives a brief explanation of why the Winter Solstice is the shortest day of the year, but this time she turned the duties over to Molly, who held up a large Christmas globe ornament from our tree inside the house.

"This is the sun," she told our gathering. Then she held up a smaller ornament in her other hand. "And this is the earth."

"Where's the moon?" Mattie asked loudly, earning a laugh but not flustering her big sister.

"Right up there," Molly said, pointing to the actual moon in the sky. "So I should say, this big globe represents the sun, and this one represents the earth. The earth's axis is tilted, and as it revolves around the sun, which takes a year to go all the way around, the tilt of the earth makes the days grow longer for six months, and then they grow shorter for six months after that. For thousands of years, humans have celebrated the time when the days begin to get longer again, for the return of the sun means more warmth for people and more sunlight for growing food."

Molly got a round of applause for her demonstration, then Susan reminded everyone that the long night is a good time to let go of troubles from the previous year by tossing something into the fire. While she explained this, she was looking directly at me.

"So long Nick," I said softly as I threw a pine cone into the fire. It was a good toss, but the pine cone must have hit a burning log, because it bounced almost straight back at me. Because Susan was watching me, everyone else was watching too, and they all laughed at my failed attempt. Anything can bounce out of the fire, but it did seem a little unusual when I tossed the pine cone a second time and it bounced out again.

"Nick's not so easy to get rid of," I thought as I picked it up again and carefully placed it into a notch in the fire.

As others tossed their own symbolic cares and woes into the flames, Linda slid up next to me and said, "Hey little brother, what were you tossing away? Whatever it was, you blew it."

I thought that was a bold statement coming from a woman with a handful of failed marriages, but then I remembered that she didn't consider them failures, and often said she was proud of every one.

"It was about Nick," I told her. "I thought I should finally quit looking for him."

"Really?" Linda said. "Funny to give up now just a few days after I saw him."

"What? You saw Nick?"

"I did indeed. He's a little older and scrawnier, but it was definitely him, white beard and all."

"Where?" I asked.

"On the Drag by campus."

"What was he doing?"

"Panhandling."

I didn't get it. What did she mean, panhandling?

"Panhandling, you know, for spare change. He looks like he's living on the street and he had a sign and was giving people little pieces of paper and asking for money."

"That's crazy," I told her. "Nick's not a bum. He wouldn't need to live on the street."

"Maybe not," she said. "But maybe yes. I mean... he practically gave you his house. Now he looks homeless. Makes sense if you think about it."

5

Jingle Bells

I DIDN'T SLEEP MUCH THAT NIGHT. LYING AWAKE, I kept thinking of Nick on the street. Was I responsible for that? If he was homeless, how I could find him? And if I found him, what was I going to do?

The sun was just coming up as I parked my car near the UT campus. Linda said she'd seen Nick sitting on the street near the University Coop store so I started there. There are plenty of homeless people in Austin, so I was surprised not to find any of them near campus. I walked several blocks up and down Guadalupe Street without any luck, and finally asked a bicycle cop if he'd seen an old homeless guy with a white beard.

"Every old homeless guy I see has a white beard," the officer told me. "But you're not going to find them out here this early."

"Why?"

"It's illegal. Austin has a no-sleeping-in-public ordinance."

"That's kind of harsh," I said, dimly remembering a public debate about this subject, one that I'd obviously not paid enough attention to. "So where do they sleep?"

"Some are down at the ARCH shelter. Families or women with kids hopefully find a program to give them safe shelter. The rest find a place to hide: down a dark alley, under a bridge, a homeless camp in the bushes in the park.

"In the park," I repeated. "Thanks."

"Hey, I don't recommend you start snooping around their home bases," the cop told me. "Check down by University Methodist church in an hour when they hand out coffee and breakfast. Maybe you'll find him there."

So I stopped into a hip coffee shop and paid five bucks for a fancy cup of coffee and wondered how we'd gotten to the point of either paying too much for something as simple as coffee or having to beg for it.

An hour later, there was a line of people waiting for coffee and food on the backside of University Methodist. It was chilly, and most of those in line were dressed in layers of clothes. I watched from across the street, and saw that they seemed to know each other in both good and bad ways. Some shared cigarettes and talked softly, but mostly they just waited for something to eat and that cup of hot coffee. The line was long and when a young guy tried to cut in at the front, the rest made a commotion and the kid shouted at them, but he still went to the back of the line.

There were a couple of older guys that bore a resemblance to Nick, so I walked across to get a better look. When I got up close, one of them turned to me quickly and said, "What are you staring at?"

His eyes were angry and he had his fists clinched. I stepped back quick and muttered an apology.

"Sorry. I thought you were someone else."

"Well, I'm not," he barked at me. "I'm me! Not somebody else. I'm me!"

I walked away and kept walking. I'd gone a couple of blocks before my heart stopped racing. I'd gotten myself into a confrontation I didn't even understand; I hadn't found Nick, and it was dawning on me that I was in over my head.

I spent the next couple of hours wandering around the fringes of the campus and finally came to Waller Creek, an urban stream that flows through parklands from campus all the way down to Lady Bird Lake. The creek passes under a lot of bridges. If Nick was homeless near campus, maybe he had a place to sleep down there.

Moving down the trail, I described him to a couple of people I came across, and asked if they'd seen him. Both asked if I had a photo of him. I didn't and never have had a photo of Nick. Even so, nearly ten years after we met, his smile and his knowing eyes are burned brightly in my mind.

I was heading downtown where the homeless congregate around various services, but along the way

I came up on a man pushing a shopping cart that was partially filled with aluminum cans. He had a little bit of white beard like Nick, but it definitely wasn't Nick, because this man's skin was black. When I came closer to talk to him, he looked at me suspiciously.

I gave him a smile and asked if he'd seen a guy that fit Nick's description and he just kept moving, stopping only when he saw a couple of cans which he tossed in the cart. I gave him more details on Nick, but he just kept walking and picking up cans. About a block from where we met, he stopped and pointed into some weeds and said, "Two cans—right there."

"What?" I asked.

"Two cans. Pick 'em up. Or is talking all you're good at?"

A little further on, he told me his name was Jasper. By then I was finding the cans myself and we were both tossing cans into the grocery cart. We went further and he stopped again.

"Listen. Since you're helping me, I don't want to lie to you," he said. "My names not really Jasper."

"So what is it?" I asked.

"I already told you, I don't want to lie to you."

"So I'll call you Jasper and you can call me Michael."

"That your real name?"

I nodded, and he laughed.

"Boy, you don't know nothing, do you? Don't ever use your real name."

"How long you been selling cans?" I asked.

"I don't know. A long time. Forever. I was a trash man—worked on a commercial truck for years but I got hurt—fell off the back, broke three vertebrae. Company insurance paid for two surgeries but the coverage ran out. Workman's comp and unemployment run out, too."

Bending over, he picked up a can and tossed it onto the cart. "Once a trash man, always a trash man. Now you're a trash man, too."

At one point we tossed in several cans that landed in a perfect rhythm and Jasper sang, "Jingle Bells, Jingle Bells."

We'd found a stash of beer cans where someone had been drinking and for a few moments, we tried to toss them into the basket on the beats of the song, with both of us singing, "Jingle bells, Jingle bells. Jingle all the way. Oh what fun it is to... fill... a one horse open sleigh."

"Not much of a sleigh," Jasper told me, "but it's all I got."

An hour later, the basket was full, and for a bunch of lightweight aluminum, it was surprisingly hard to push. Jasper told me to watch it for him, then he disappeared down a dirt trail towards the creek. In a minute, he came back with a second cart and we continued on our journey, collecting more cans and telling stories.

I don't know why, but I told him about my brother dying on Christmas Day, me just a kid looking back at the broken ice from the shore where David slid me to, him taking the plunge into the cold instead of me. We stopped picking up cans while I finished the story, then Jasper came over and wrapped his arms around me and gave me a long hug. It was uncomfortable at first, but then it felt good.

"Why you looking for this Nick fella?" Jasper asked. "He family?"

I told him how I'd hated Christmas for years, and how Nick had rekindled the love of the holiday in me and helped save my son.

"Christmas always makes me sad," Jasper told me. "Maybe I need to find old St. Nick myself."

It was getting warm out, and when I picked up a can, a bee flew out of it and flew straight at my eyes. I jerked my face to one side, but only quick enough for the bee to sting me on my cheek.

"Ow!" I called out in pain.

Jasper ran over to me to check it out, and asked me if I was allergic. I told him I didn't think so, and he asked me if I had a credit card.

So there it is, I thought. I lend someone a hand, get stung by a bee, can't see very well and there goes my credit card.

"Why?" I asked suspiciously.

"Just give it to me," Jasper said.

Taking the card, he laid it against my cheek, slid it up to the bee stinger, then dropped a thumbnail on the other side and pulled the tiny stinger out.

"Look how small," he said, handing back the credit card with the little stinger on it. "Hard to believe it hurts that much, hunh?"

"You get stung often?" I asked.

"Oh yeah. Four or five times a day when the weather's warm. Bees and wasps love Coca Cola. The Yellow Jackets hurt the worst. A hazard of the trade."

It took us a while to push two full carts under I-35 to the metal recycling yard where the guy in charge told Jasper he was late. Jasper hitched a thumb in my direction, blaming his slow pace on me, then the man weighed the cans, printed a receipt, and counted out some cash.

"How much?" I asked.

"Eighty pounds. Twenty-four dollars," Jasper told me. "Price is going down. Getting to be, it don't pay to be homeless."

Counting the money twice to make sure he hadn't been short-changed, Jasper held out some of the bills to me.

"You want half?" he asked.

"No, thanks. I just slowed you down."

We shook hands and said good-bye. As I was walked away, Jasper called after me.

"Hey. If you can't find your friend, chances are he don't want to be found."

River

BY THE TIME I WALKED BACK TO MY CAR AND drove home, I was tired from walking and sore from bending over and pushing that cart, plus my face was swollen from the bee sting. I'd covered a lot of ground, and though I hadn't found Nick, I had no regrets. When I told Susan about Jasper and the cans, her reaction was more muted than I expected.

"Is this a one-time thing?" she asked. "Or are you going to make friends with every homeless person in Austin?"

I didn't have an answer for that question, not when she asked it and not even by dinner when I was thinking I should make one more drive around town before dark. It was an unusual family dinner because the whole conversation centered on my day wandering the streets of Austin, which David and little Mattie thought was awesome, and which Susan thought was futile, and Molly seemed to think was just plain dumb.

I didn't expect everyone to be all gung-ho, but I did want them to understand my reasons.

"I know I might not find Nick," I explained. "Or like Jasper said, maybe he doesn't want me to find him. Maybe he's bitter that he sold us the house too cheap. Maybe he's ashamed that he's homeless. Maybe he really is St. Nick. I don't know. But we've been incredibly fortunate to call this place home, and I don't think anyone should take their blessings for granted, especially at Christmas."

When I finished my little speech, I looked around the table, from Susan to David to Molly to Mattie, and the looks on their faces made me feel very loved.

"Dad, we hope you find him," Molly told me. "Then we'll finally know what his racket is."

Having pushed me as far as a teenager is likely to get away with, she excused herself and made up for her general level of sarcasm by doing what she did every night after dinner—going straight to the piano. She started to play *Jingle Bells*, but that just turned out to be the intro to Joni Mitchell's pensive Christmas song *River*, the only Christmas song with lyrics that rhyme "cutting down trees" with "singing songs of joy and peace."

Outside our front door, the sky was dark and up and down Wonderland Avenue, the lights were shining bright as throngs of strangers wandered past our house. We didn't get up to go join them, for we had our own Christmas celebration going on right where we were.

When Molly finished playing, I asked David how

the college applications were going.

"Good," he told me. "Still no word from Harvard, but I applied to Yale, Princeton, Stanford, MIT and Cornell. All great schools but somehow they seem like settling."

"They'd be crazy not to fight for you," Susan told him.

"No matter which school you go to," I said. "Next year I'll be putting up Christmas lights without you. I haven't done that since the year we bought the house."

"Dad, you ever think about letting the lights go?" David asked. "Maybe just do a few strings on the big pine tree and skip the rest?"

"That could be a good idea," Susan added. "So many neighbors have already quit."

"It is a good idea, but I can't do it."

"Why?" David and Susan both asked.

"Because I promised Nick."

"Good!" Mattie chimed in. "If we don't have lots of Christmas lights, how will Santa find our house?"

When Molly finished playing, she started giving Mattie a piano lesson, so David and I took a walk and checked on our neighbors. When I'd first come to Wonderland Avenue, most of the residents sat on their porches during the light fest nights, waving and chatting with the people passing by. This year, David and I covered the first two blocks and didn't see one person we knew.

I did see two different guys who I briefly thought

might be Nick. And we stopped to listen to an old-timey barbershop quartet. All sporting handlebar mustaches, they had a sled in front of them with a sign that said, "Wish us a Merry Christmas!" The sled was half-filled with tips. Further on, a guy was playing *The First Noël* on a musical saw. He had a carpenter's wooden tool box for a tip jar. The sign on the toolbox read, "Jesus was a carpenter."

Most of the crowd's attention was going to a group of partying college students in biblical-looking clothing. They were led by a costumed Joseph and Mary, the latter of which had her belly padded to look like a full pregnancy. Joseph and Mary were knocking on doors and asking if there was room at the inn, and the young men with them, all wearing long robes, were drinking beer while doing their best to move a herd of actual sheep from house to house.

David and I exchanged a worried look because we both knew the group was only two doors from Mrs. Bumgarten, the hermit of Live Oak Lane who a couple of years earlier had replaced her Christmas lights with signs that said "Keep Off the Grass" and "Don't Trample my Flowers."

Winters have been growing progressively warmer in Austin for as long as anyone can remember, and the number of really cold days has shrunk to the point that you can pretty much play golf or swim at Barton Springs year-round. We still get a couple of cold snaps with lows in the teens, but you can cover a flower or vegetable bed for a few nights and have a beautiful, blooming garden throughout the year.

Sensing trouble for Mrs. Bumgarten's pansies, David and I moved ahead of the sheep Posada and stood guard on the flowers. I knew we were unlikely to succeed when Joseph and Mary rang the doorbell of the Trejo family next door. Choosing exactly the wrong house to get silly, when Jesus Trejo opened the door, Mary blurted out "Trick or Treat!" and all the shepherds cracked up laughing.

Jesus looked from the very fake and not very respectful Joseph and Mary to the laughing sheepherders, who were all holding beers, then slammed the door in their faces.

No matter, they all laughed and headed straight for David and me and Mrs. Bumgarten's pansies.

"Hold on," I told them. "You need to go around this house."

As the sheep and sheepherders pushed by me, I tried a little sterner warning, one based on previous experience.

"She'll call the cops," I warned.

Despite David's and my efforts to push the sheep off the flowerbed, half the pansies were gone in three minutes, nipped off at ground level. A number of others were adorning Mary's hair and scarf as she and Joseph rang Mrs. Bumgarten's doorbell.

"What do we do?" David asked me.

At that moment, the door swung open, and Mrs.

Bumgarten stepped out with a shotgun in her hand. It took about three seconds for the entire street to fall quiet.

"I'm having lamb chops for dinner!" Mrs. Bumgarten said as she cocked both barrels of the shotgun.

"Run!" I told David, but maybe not before Joseph, Mary, the sheepherders and everyone else were already dashing away. Having tried to pull the sheep off the flowers, we were standing right in the middle of them as she leveled the shotgun at the biggest ram, placed her cheek along the stock for better aim, then pulled the trigger which clicked loudly on an empty chamber.

"Merry &%@! Christmas!" Mrs. Bumgarten called out to the retreating crowd.

"Let's call it a night," I said to David when I could breathe again.

"Good idea," he said.

7

Santa Baby

THE NEXT DAY WAS GOOD GROWING WEATHER for the recovery of Mrs. Bumgarten's pansies. It was almost too hot to walk and search for Nick, so I spent a couple of hours driving around town, hitting the major intersections where panhandlers were holding signs with all kinds of holiday messages.

On the prosperous West side of town, the signs had clever messages: "Be Santa for a Day," "Fill my Stocking" and "It's Better to Give Than Receive."

As I moved further to the east side, the signs and the holders seemed more grim—a woman with a sign that read, "Anything Helps," then a teenager that looked completely wasted with a shortened version that read, "Anything." And finally a young man who had no legs and sat forlornly in a wheel chair with a sign that simply read, "Help."

I saw drivers handing them money and sometimes a bottle of water or something to eat. I handed out some of all three, but never met anyone who knew an old guy named Nick.

With just three days left till Christmas, I was

feeling down about the prospects of finding him. When I got home, Susan tried to cheer me up by saying I'd done everything I could. She also reminded me that the kids were out of school for the holidays and I hadn't been spending much time with them.

Determined to do better, the next morning I took the whole family to breakfast at Kerbey Lane, an old Austin cafe with fluffy pancakes, huge omelets, and big cups of coffee that don't cost five bucks. After breakfast, I suggested we stop by the street market at UT and do some last minute shopping.

"Good idea," David told me. "We can help you look for Nick while we're there."

I could see that Susan had the same thought as David, but in not so positive a light. Either way, they all knew I had an extra motive to go there.

The official name for the artist area on the UT Drag is the Renaissance Market. It's been there as long as I can remember, the artists setting up displays of their hand-made items in designated spots. There's hand-blown glass, jewelry, custom leatherwork amd hand-made journals. Most of the vendors have been selling there for years, and a license is required, so there's not really room for unofficial vendors. Like most jobs, homeless people need not apply.

It's tricky to buy Christmas presents when your family is with you. We keep the gift giving simple in the Walker household, and I wanted to see what the others admired because I hadn't done any shopping and also didn't have any ideas. So I tagged along behind the kids and eavesdropped as best I could, then looped back a couple of times to make a small purchase.

Susan was more or less doing the same, then I realized the kids were, too. We circled each other for an hour or so, and when we gathered to leave, there was one thing missing—one very important thing—Mattie.

Losing your 5-year-old girl at a crowded outdoor market is not recommended. The four of us all started talking at once, trying to figure who was with her last. After about 10 seconds, I said, "Split up and look!"

We all went different directions. The market's only one block long and there are maybe three dozen vendors, so it didn't take long to determine she wasn't there. We were about to go up and down the adjacent streets when Susan's hand flew into the air.

"There she is!"

Sure enough, Mattie was coming down the sidewalk toward us with a big smile on her face. We ran to her and all started talking at once.

"Are you okay?" "Don't wander off." "You scared us."

"I was close," she said casually. "Right over there. And look, someone gave me a Christmas present."

Opening her hand, she showed us a beautiful origami Christmas tree, folded with precision on a green piece of paper.

"Wow!" David said. "That's cool."

"Who?" Susan asked her little girl. "Who gave it to you?

"A man. He's sitting over there. He's old and he has a white beard like Daddy's friend. Let's go say hi. I think it's Santa Nick!"

We'd only gone a short ways down the sidewalk when Mattie pointed at a recessed doorway.

"He's right there," she said.

We came around the corner, but there was no one there. Looking up quickly, I checked both ways to see if I could spot him.

"He was here," Mattie said. "He asked if I'd been a good girl, and he gave me this little tree. Was it Santa Nick?"

"I don't know," I told her. "But I'm glad you're okay."

8

God Rest Ye Merry Gentlemen

CHRISTMAS EVE DAWNED CLEAR AND COLD, AND the morning news had footage of long lines of homeless men and women lined up at the ARCH, a one-stop shop for all kinds of assistance to the homeless, but which Jasper and others had told me has too many sketchy people and shady deals. The number of people who crowd around the facility also make it a thorn in the side of some downtown business owners, who seem to hope the homeless would simply go away.

With a deep freeze forecast for Christmas Eve, the staff at the ARCH was going to be a hard-pressed finding sleeping space for everyone. But if most of Austin's homeless were headed there, I figured Nick might be doing the same.

After circling the block, I parked and walked to the line that was all men and spoke up loud enough that a whole section of them could hear me.

"Any of you guys know my friend Nick? Old guy with white hair and a beard?"

"I do!" said one of the guys. "Tell you where he is for twenty bucks."

"I know him," said another. "I'll tell you for ten."

"Five bucks," said another, and they all burst into laughter.

I was in it now. Who was I to them? Just a guy with more money than they had. After a moment, the first guy came up close to me, then leaned closer still, and said, "Why don't you just give us all five bucks and we'll call it even."

I stood there for a second trying to decide what to say or do, and whether I could just turn around and walk away. Then a voice from the far end said, "What's wrong with you guys? It's Christmas for Christ's sake!"

The big voice belonged to a little guy who came up to rescue me.

"Listen. For all we know, you're a cop or some other bad news. Nobody here is gonna help you because the last things we need here are cops and tourists."

Back in my car where the searching felt safer, I looped around several parks and wherever else I could remember that I'd seen homeless people.I didn't find Nick, but a couple of hours later, I saw Jasper again. He was south of the river, pulling cans from the trash cans at a parking lot for the hike and bike trail. I rolled down my window and whistled to him.

"Was hoping I'd see you," I said. "Brought you something."

He smiled when he recognized me, and smiled wider when I opened my trunk and showed him ten grocery bags full of aluminum cans that David had picked up along Wonderland Avenue after a crowded weekend of the light fest.

"Wow," Jasper said, "I don't think all that's gonna fit in my cart."

"Put your cans in with mine and I'll drive you to the metal yard. Long way around from this side of the river."

"What about my cart?"

"Stash it and I'll bring you back."

Fifteen minutes later, we'd doubled Jasper's usual take, and he had fifty dollars for his and David's cans combined. Just as he was cashing out, the wind switched around to the north and the temps seemed to drop twenty degrees.

"Gonna be a cold one tonight," Jasper said as we were driving back to his cart.

"My Gramma Jean would have called this cold front a 'blue norther,'" I told him. "So, you got a warm place to sleep?"

"I'm okay," he reassured me. "Got me a place in a garage on the Eastside. Fellow I know lets me sleep in the back seat of his old car in there. It don't run, but I've got blankets to keep me warm and a car charger thing I found that lets me run the radio. There's a garden hose so I've got running water."

"You got any family?"

"A sister in California; and a son. He's a good boy but he's in prison right now. Never seemed like the type to get in trouble, but I guess you never know."

I wrote my name and phone number on a piece of paper and handed it to him. "You need anything, you call me; help you find a job, whatever. Okay?"

"Okay," he said as he got out to retrieve his cart. But then he turned back to me.

"One more thing, Mr. Walker," he said, reading my name on the paper.

"Michael," I reminded him.

"One more thing, Michael. I think I know where your friend Nick is. Don't know exactly, but I heard he stays over on the West side. Lots of bridges and overpasses by the train track and freeway there. Keeps you out of the rain, but that concrete gets cold. That ain't no place for an old man on a cold night."

I thanked Jasper and headed that direction. It seemed like it was getting colder by the minute, so I turned on the radio and heard the weatherman talking nonsense about the possibility of a white Christmas, something the forecasters muse about every year, even though Austin hasn't seen a white Christmas in fifty years. Even without snow, it was going to be close to 20 degrees, dangerous weather for anyone sleeping outside.

"It's gonna be a cold night out for old Saint Nick," the weatherman concluded.

"Not if I can help it," I mumbled.

The streets under the MoPac highway intersection loop in a lot of funny ways. There's a railroad track, bridges, overpasses that carry traffic into town and underpasses that carry it out. There's hike and bike trails with their own bridges, some in use and some abandoned. I made half a dozen slow loops as close as I could go in my car. Then I parked and walked through looking in every corner I could find. I was shivering in a light jacket as the wind howled out of the north. And I didn't see any sign of Nick.

Maybe Jasper had been mistaken, I thought. In any event, it was getting dark and my family was sitting at home on Christmas Eve without me. I'd given it my best and I felt like I'd gotten close, but finally had to admit that I couldn't find Nick. Maybe I was being stupid to think I could so easily correct the course of his life.

So I went home, still thinking about Nick all the way.

9

Santa Claus is Coming to Town

I TRIED TO BE A GOOD CHRISTMAS EVE DAD. I BUILT a fire in the fireplace. I sat next to Molly at the piano and sang Christmas carols with my family. I made popcorn in the kitchen. It was lovely, but I kept thinking it had been Nick's fireplace, Nick's piano and Nick's kitchen.

I knew it was probably pointless to go searching again. If I couldn't find Nick in eleven warm days, chances were I wouldn't succeed on one cold night. But I couldn't stop looking at the temperature on the thermometer outside the kitchen window, and was constantly checking my phone for weather info.

When Mattie heard there was a possibility of a white Christmas, she was beyond excited. Not only had she never seen snow on Christmas Day, she'd never even seen snow. We turned on the ten o'clock news to watch the forecast and the weatherman showed us a NORAD radar track with an object flying across the sky from the North Pole.

"There's Santa Nick!" Mattie hollered. "No wonder you couldn't find him."

The actual radar had something equally amazing and showed the progress of a large band of snow and sleet as it moved through the Texas Hill Country toward Austin.

When the forecast was over, I got my heaviest coat and a warm cap and I told Susan I'd be back as soon as I could.

"I'm surprised you stayed this long," she said, giving me a kiss. "Good luck. And Merry Christmas."

LET ME TELL YOU, IT WAS COLD AND IT WAS WINDY. When I opened the front door, I wasn't sure I could get it closed again. It had been below freezing for a couple of hours, so the wind chill was pushing the single digits.

When I got home from my afternoon search under the MoPac bridges, I'd gone online and found several maps of Austin's hike and bike trails. They've done a lot of construction in that area, and I noticed that there were a couple of loops of the trail on the older maps that no longer showed on the new ones. Those two sections were my last hope. I parked at El Arroyo, a Mexican restaurant affectionately referred to as "The Ditch" for the drainage ditch or *arroyo* that runs beneath it. The restaurant was closed but their magnetic letter sign by the street, famous for its daily witty sayings, simply said, "Merry Christmas to all, and to all a good night!"

I had to climb a fence to get to the first section of closed trail. It wasn't hard. A lot of people had climbed it and bent it half-over. When I got to the other side, I turned on my flashlight and discovered this was an outdoor toilet for whoever needed one. It was a mess and I was glad the wind was carrying the smell away from me.

I climbed back over the fence and made a loop to where I thought the other spot was. The fence there was taller and sturdier, no easy way through for me, and certainly not for a guy in his 70's or maybe older than that.

I was about to give up when the wind died for a moment and I heard someone cough, a deep, raspy rattle of a cough. After a bit, I heard it again just before the wind carried the sound away.

I started pushing and pulling on the fence, looking for a way through. There was a tall, rusted gate, but I'd already checked and found it locked by a heavy chain and padlock. Since I couldn't find another way, I went back and pulled on the padlock. There was something familiar about it, and then I realized it was the same kind of lock that was still on my storeroom behind the house. That was a lock Nick had left behind.

I shined my light on the four little dials on the bottom and they were set to 2-6-0-1. The lock at our house was the same as our street address on Live Oak Lane—2600. Taking off a glove, I dialed the 1 to a 0 and pulled on the lock. When it opened, I knew I'd found Nick.

10

Baby It's Cold Outside

TWENTY FEET BACK FROM THE GATE AND ONLY partially sheltered from the wind, there was a pile of thin blankets and a beard that looked like it had once been white.

"Nick. Is that you?" I asked.

He looked up slowly, a tired and broken man. When he saw my face, there was a flicker of recognition that brought a light to his eyes.

"Michael. It's been a long time."

"Yes it has. Too long."

"How's your son?"

"He's good, Nick. I think the real question is, how are you?"

I waited for an answer.

"I've been better," Nick finally said. "I never much cared for cold weather, which is kinda ironic for old St. Nick." He laughed at that, and that made him start coughing again.

I didn't know what to do. Just standing there, I was getting colder by the minute and couldn't imagine how he must feel.

"Let's go to the house," I said. But when I tried to help him up, he pulled back from my touch.

"Can't do that," he mumbled. "Not like this."

I hadn't expected pride to be an issue, but I did have another idea. We were only a short drive from an all-night diner that serves a late night mix of musicians and insomniacs. I'd never seen a homeless person in there, or in any other Austin restaurant for that matter, but I knew it would be warm. What I didn't know was that the 24-hour restaurant was closing for Christmas. Seeing us coming and perhaps not wanting to lose any of his own holiday time, a waiter flipped the sign to "Closed." The door was still unlocked, so I went in and explained Nick's situation to the manager, basically saying it was a matter of life and death to get him warm and get some food inside him.

The manager sent some of the staff home and found a booth for us. "After all, it's almost Christmas," he said.

Nick had hardly spoken, but when he took his first sip of hot coffee, he looked up at me and said, "Thank you."

My elation at finally finding him had carried me through so far, but those two words nearly did me in. I was sure this was all my fault. Nick had rescued us from the verge of being homeless ourselves, and had rescued me from an emotional poverty as well. At the time, I'd thought he'd accomplished those miracles by magic, with the wave of his hand and a twinkle in his eye, but now I knew that our gain had been his sacrifice.

He'd helped me learn to love Christmas again, as I had as a child. I'd learned to smile and to sing again, but I hadn't learned the true meaning—the obligations and the opportunities—of Christmas.

It had been so much easier and more fun to say he was Santa Claus, a magical and mythical Christmas apparition who'd built it all for us before sleighing back to the North Pole. He was a legend in our family and for other families who'd heard or read my story. Good old Nick. Good old St. Nick.

He had both hands wrapped around his coffee cup. As I watched his labored breathing, I wondered if I should have taken him to the hospital instead of a cafe.

"You okay?" I asked again.

He nodded slowly and did his best to give me a smile. "Kinda cold out there."

I ordered eggs and pancakes for both of us, then we just sat there, neither one of us knowing what to say.

After a while, Nick broke the silence.

"It's Christmas Eve. You should be with your family."

"They'll wait," I said.

"They're all okay?"

"Better than okay. We've done well in your house."

"Good. That's why I sold it to you."

After another long silence, I worked up my nerve

and said, "Why? Why did you sell us your home for so little money?"

He looked me in the eye and for one second I saw a flash of that Nick I'd met all those years ago.

"It was all you could afford. Besides, you needed it more than me."

It was quickly becoming clear that if I needed Nick to absolve me of my guilt, I might be on a futile quest.

"Doesn't matter," he told me. "Doesn't matter that I sold it, or what I sold it for. I was ready to go. More money would've just been more money to give away."

I was trying to figure out what he meant when the pancakes arrived. They were fluffy and steaming, and I watched with pleasure as he ate a couple of big bites.

"Good," he told me. "Heavenly. Say, I'm not dead, am I?"

"No, you're just in pancake heaven," I said.

We both laughed, and for the first time, I was confident Nick was going to make it.

So I told him about my family, about David who loves basketball and medicine, about Molly the sarcastic teenager who thought he was a con but played Nick's beautiful piano like an angel, and about our baby girl, Mattie, who loves to laugh. He drank it all in like hot coffee and said, "That makes me happy."

I also told him about the street he'd lived on, and how all the attention to the lights and Christmas atmosphere had slowly stripped away the magic.

"Too many people, too much liquid cheer instead

of Christmas cheer," I said. "It got really got bad after we were featured in Oprah's Christmas special, *Oprah in Wonderland.*"

Nick looked up and said, "So you're telling me that Oprah..."

"That's right. Oprah killed Christmas!"

We both laughed again.

"And you're still putting up your lights?" he asked.

I nodded and said, "Your turn. What happened? How'd you end up on the street like all those other guys?

"Not just guys," he told me. "Women too. And families. And kids. That's the worst of it."

"I know. I've seen it."

"You see it, but you don't get it. I'm not out there with those other people. I'm out there alone. Just like they are. Somewhere along the way, we all lost our families. Some through tragedy or divorce; some through neglect, some from drugs and booze, some can't read or don't know how to play the game."

"What game?"

"What else? Life. I'm not trying to excuse the booze or the drugs, but for many, that's all they got left. You think I regret selling you my house, but you're wrong. I screwed up a lot of things after I sold it to you. I got caught up in pretending to be St. Nick and pretty much gave it all away. House, truck, money. I should've made the money last, but selling you that house was the smartest thing I ever did."

I didn't know what to say, so I didn't say anything.

Warm now, Nick unbuttoned his heavy coat and another one underneath it. Reaching to an inside pocket, he pulled out a wallet.

"You're not paying for this," I told him.

He smiled and took out a newspaper clipping, the Austin paper with a photo of my family on the front porch of our home all lit up in Christmas lights.

"Look at that," he said. "That's what I keep over my heart. We're not family but I still have someone to care about, and I know that a lot of good things for you and for others have happened because of me."

"We are family," I told him. "And we have a place for you."

"We'll see," Nick told me. "We'll see."

As the waitress poured more coffee, Nick smiled and said, "Merry Christmas, Michael."

I looked at the time, one minute after midnight, and said, "Merry Christmas."

"Wish me a happy birthday," he said.

"What? It's not really your birthday, is it? You were born on Christmas Day?"

"Oh yeah. Born on Christmas and my dad thought it would be perfect to name me for St. Nick. I hated that Christmas birthday when I was growing up. All the other kids got presents twice, on their birthday and on Christmas, too. But Christmas birthday kids only get presents once. My classmates called me St. Nick and they wrote Christmas wish lists and gave them to me all through December. And I pretty much dreaded the entire month."

"What happened to change that?" I asked.

"My dad died. Don't freak out—it wasn't on Christmas Day like your brother. He just worked too hard and had a heart attack way too young. I missed him, and I decided Christmas was the best way to honor him. So we share something, you and me."

I still didn't know what to say.

"I married a woman who loved Christmas, too, and we celebrated Christmas in a big way," Nick said. "It was great for a long time, but then it lost its magic."

"Is that when we met?"

"Earlier. By the time we met, I was ready to go."

"So are you ready to go see the house?"

"I don't know. Look at me. Your kids shouldn't see me like this."

"Well I'm not putting you back in the cold to freeze to death, and they're not gonna let you spend the night here, so looks like you're coming home whether you like it or not."

When I asked for the check, the manager said to forget it, it was his treat. And then the waitress and the cook came up behind Nick. Somebody had been eavesdropping because they were carrying a big slice of cake with candles, and started singing "Happy Birthday" to a homeless Santa born eighty years earlier on Christmas Day.

When they came to the end of the song, they didn't know Nick's name, so they just sang, "Happy birthday dear Santa. Happy birthday to you."

11

Silent Night

IT WAS 1 A.M. WHEN NICK AND I DROVE DOWN Wonderland Avenue, mostly dark with the exception of Nick's old house where the Christmas lights were still shining like a beacon. I didn't say a word as we got out of the car, and just watched Nick as his gaze panned across it all.

The cold weather had stuck the front door tightly closed, an annual problem. I pushed on it with no success, then Nick reached forward to the handle.

"Lift it a little, then push. It doesn't like the cold either."

And with the slightest effort, he pushed the door open and went into his home for the first time in ten years.

Hearing the door, Susan ran to greet me.

"We were worried..." she said, but then she saw Nick, looking exactly like he'd been sleeping in the woods for weeks, and her words trailed away.

"I'm sorry I didn't call," I told her. "My phone died."

The kids were playing a board game in front of the fire while they waited for me. When they looked up and saw Nick, there was a long silence.

"Sorry to interrupt," Nick said softly.

Mattie stood up and came closer, looking up at Nick, who didn't look much like Santa Claus, and said. "Are you Santa Nick?"

"That all depends," he told her in a weak voice. "You folks mind if I wash up for a minute?"

"Of course, the bathroom is..." Then I trailed off, feeling like a fool. "I guess you know where the bathroom is."

Nick went in and Susan and the kids surrounded me, peppering me with questions.

"Where did you find him?"

"Are you okay?"

"Did you give him any money?"

This went on for a while, ending only with Nick surprising us by saying, "I'm fine. I'm fine. Merry Christmas one and all."

Our gazes turned in his direction and our mouths fell open. He'd cleaned up well. The greasy grime in his beard and hair were gone. Both were white as snow. His two old coats were off and he was wearing a red sweater. Here indeed was the Nick who we'd so long thought of as St. Nick.

Nick smiled, came closer and leaned down to Mattie. "What's your name?" he asked. "Is it Mattie?"

"You are Santa Nick!" Mattie said with wonder.

"Not so fast," he told her. "What do you know about Santa Claus?"

"He lives at the North Pole where it's very cold."

"Okay, then I at least feel like Santa Claus."

"And Santa Claus has reindeer," Mattie continued. "He brings toys to kids who've been good."

"Have you been good?" he asked as he sat on the sofa. "If you've been good, Santa will likely bring you something special. Did you ask for anything special from Santa?"

Mattie nodded a yes, then climbed onto the sofa, leaned close, and whispered in his ear.

Hearing her wish, Nick's eyes lit up. Then holding her at arm's length so he could focus on her, he said, "Mattie, my name is Nick, and I have never wished I was Santa Claus more than at this very moment. But let me tell you something very important about Santa Claus."

"What?"

"You have to be asleep for him to find you."

I should probably add that Mattie, despite being five-years-old, is essentially a night person. Getting her to sleep has been a constant challenge, as is waking her up in the morning. Looking skeptically at Nick, she considered his words and said, "Really?"

"Really," Nick told her.

And just like that, she gave him a kiss on the cheek and said, "Goodnight Nick. Good night everyone." And she went off to bed.

A little dumbfounded, we watched her go into the hall and up the stairs.

"So David," Nick said, "how you been?

David didn't say a word. 18 years old and ready

for college, he'd been hearing me talk about Nick for half his life without once meeting him. Still, Nick's Christmas spirit had helped us overcome David's sorrow when his grandfather was killed in the car accident. All these years later, a guy who looks like a bum stumbles in the door on Christmas Eve, then reappears looking like the very spirit of Christmas, with a little wear around the edges. This was a far cry from years of thinking of Nick as a knight in a shiny Santa suit, and I saw David glance from Nick to his pile of dirty clothes and belongings.

When David couldn't respond, Molly rescued him.

"What'd my sister say she wanted for Christmas?" she asked. It was clear that she thought something fishy was going on. "Mattie gets her hopes up high and it doesn't look like you've been doing much Christmas shopping."

"What Mattie said is a secret!" Nick said, ignoring Molly's tone. "But you're right, I have neglected my Christmas shopping."

This conversation was going nowhere so Susan interrupted and said, "Maybe it's time for us to all get some sleep."

"But..." Nick interrupted. "What if there really was a Santa Claus. What would you ask for, David?"

"There's no Santa Claus," Molly answered for her brother. Mattie is the only one in this house who doesn't know that."

"But if there was," said Nick. "Surely there'd be

something you wanted, Molly. And you, too, David. I don't mean a car or anything crazy like that."

"A scholarship to Harvard," David told him flatly. "Do you have four years of college you can float down the chimney?"

"Not that chimney," Nick said with a laugh, pointing at the roaring fire I'd stoked. "I'm afraid it'd burn up! But I've got a feeling you'll get that scholarship anyway. Good night son. And good luck with your studies. And good night to you, Molly. Maybe I'll get to hear you play that old piano sometime."

As David was going up to his room, Susan brought in a blanket and a pillow for Nick. She set them next to him on the sofa, and Nick said, "A red blanket. Would you look at that?"

The two of them said good night and I said it was probably time for Nick and me to get some sleep, too.

Before I could leave, Nick said, "You split the firewood just like I used to."

I looked at the blazing logs and thought about how much time I'd spent splitting them.

"The split firewood you left behind lasted two years. I tried the easy way for the next two winters, using sawn logs but not splitting them, but the fire wasn't the same. Kept going out or the wood didn't burn right, so I started splitting logs. I've tried to do things the way you did them, but it's a lot of house. I'm not sure how successful I've been."

"Looks like you've done all right," Nick told me.

"But I don't see many presents under that tree."

"I've been busy," I told him, not mentioning that I'd been busy looking for him. "Besides, the kids don't ask for much. We just do one present each. And maybe something extra from Santa for Mattie."

"Mattie had a small Santa wish," he confided, "but she also whispered that she's too old to believe in Santa."

"Maybe. But she still believes in Santa's presents. Who they come from is not a big concern."

Giving me a big Nick smile, he said, "You know, when kids write their Christmas list to Santa, what they write reveals their parents' characters. Lots of asks and wishes probably mean that, just like their parents, they'll never have enough stuff. Kinda heart-breaking when you think about it. Ninety percent of all Christmas presents are just junk—just a laugh when you unwrap 'em: a kitchen gadget that disappears into a drawer, a tie that won't be worn, a toy that might fly once."

"It's a complicated holiday," I added, "giving and getting all rolled into one."

"True, true," he told me. "I always liked the old-school way—exchange gifts you made. A present made by your loved one's hand—now that's a true gift."

I went to the bookshelf and pulled down a small, carved, wooden Christmas tree and handed it to Nick.

"David gave that to me when he was 13."

Nick looked at it closely, spinning it slowly. He even smelled the wood.

"Yeah, that's a real treasure," he said.

"Lemme ask you something, Michael. Something serious."

"Shoot."

"You got any whiskey?"

"You sure you should be drinking?"

"Not for me," he said. "It's for you. So you'll quit looking at me like that."

"Like what?"

"Like you ruined my life. A man makes decisions, good or bad; what makes him a man is he learns to live by them. There's not enough time in life for regret. I made decisions and then I found out where they led me. And they were my decisions, not yours. So get that whiskey. You need a drink."

I started to the kitchen but before I got there, he said, "I just made another decision. Bring two glasses."

So we sat in front of the fire we'd both made, and we drank a whiskey—or two—and Nick told me about his life the past ten years, about meeting a mom with big medical bills, and about a nice man who needed a pick-up truck for his business but didn't have the money to buy one."

"And you sold him yours for half of what it was worth?" I added.

"You got the picture," Nick told me.

He told me about a garage apartment he rented,

a job that he took to help a family out, about some of the people he met who helped him and who he helped, too. But none of it helped him with his struggle to do the one thing he seemed to be completely incapable of doing, which was to enjoy life without his wife of 40 years. They'd never had kids, and when she died, he was truly alone.

"Christmas got me by for a while after she passed," Nick confided. "Christmas on this magical street with my neighbors did the trick for one month every year. But in the long run, it wasn't enough."

I didn't know what to say, except that I was truly sorry for his loss. While we sat for a moment in silence, I heard soft footsteps on the stairs and realized how late it was. Susan was coming down to tell us to go to sleep.

But it wasn't Susan. In a few seconds, we heard the piano as Molly began to play *Silent Night.* She'd come back to fulfill Nick's Christmas wish.

We listened to every note, both of us nodding softly in appreciation. When she finished, we heard her footsteps going back up to bed, then I picked up the whiskey to put it away.

"Hold on," Nick said. "You didn't ask what I want for Christmas."

"I didn't, but I thought about it," I said. "We were thinking, it would be a good Christmas if Susan and I fixed up that old apartment behind the garage, and you moved in with us. You'd have a place that was really your home, and you could help out around here... when you felt like it."

"That's what *you* want," Nick told me. "That's what you want for Christmas."

So I sat back down and said, "Maybe you're right. So what do you want?"

"I don't know," Nick told me. "I'm really tired. Maybe I just want to get some sleep."

He pulled the red blanket over him and mumbled a good night. Before I'd left the room, he was sleeping soundly, home at last.

I went up to bed and I dreamt about Christmas with my grandparents and my brother in the mountains of New Mexico all those years ago. It was a beautiful dream. After so many years, I was with my big brother David once again.

The sun was coming up when I awoke on a beautiful Christmas morning. I went down to the living room, and Nick was gone.

12

Little Drummer Boy

Despite the cold weather and the optimistic forecast, the snow never made it to Austin. Having stayed up late, we let Mattie sleep until the sun streamed in the window of her bedroom.

I was making coffee and wondering what I'd said wrong and where Nick could have gone when Mattie came downstairs excitedly, saying "Wake up! It's Christmas morning!"

Nick had folded the red blanket. He'd washed the whiskey glasses and left them by the sink. And he'd taken his old coats and his bag of stuff with him. I went into the living room to explain to Mattie that he'd had to leave early, but she cut me off.

"He was Santa! Santa was in our house!" she said excitedly. "I told him I wanted a reindeer and a red drum, and look!" Then she opened her hand and showed me a nearly perfect origami reindeer, almost impossibly beautiful, folded with care and skill out of the colored gift-wrapping that Susan had left by the tree.

"That's a treasure," I said to Mattie. Then I noticed

that she was glancing around the room and knew why almost immediately. She'd asked Santa for two presents and gotten one.

"Sometimes Christmas presents show up a day or two late," I told her.

Having heard the commotion, Molly had joined us and also joined in.

"Mattie," she said, "Sometimes people say whatever it takes to get what they need, even if it's just a place to get warm."

Mattie nodded her head and gave her sister a weak smile. "Sometimes," she said.

Now Susan was standing in the doorway, two cups of coffee in her hands and a puzzled look in her eyes. With a nod of her head, she beckoned me to come to her.

"What's wrong?" I asked. Unable to find any words, she nodded her head again, this time towards the music room.

"Did you do that?" she finally asked.

Coming through the doorway, my eyes grew wide. There beside Nick's grand piano was a little stand and a beautiful red drum.

"Not me," I said.

Hearing that, Mattie came running over, saw the drum and shouted for joy.

"I knew it, I knew it, I knew it!" she said. "Santa Nick brought me a drum!"

My mind reeled. Mattie hadn't told Susan or me she wanted a drum. And even when she told Nick, how could he have found one in the middle of night with every store closed? One answer kept coming to my mind, but it was an answer that no adult believes in.

By then, Mattie had found the drumsticks on the drum and was playing her favorite Christmas song, *Little Drummer Boy.*

Tum tum-tum-tum-tum-tum, she played several times in a row. Finally Molly took the hint and sat at the piano and the two of them played the song, with David and Susan joining in to sing.

Come they told me. Pa rum pum pum pum
A newborn King to see. Pa rum pum pum pum
Our finest gifts to bring. Pa rum pum pum pum
To lay before a King. Pa rum pum pum pum

As they sang, my emotions washed over me, and I kept asking myself, "How?" But as Mattie got more accustomed to the drum, the music washed away my doubts like a river, and I raised my voice with the others and sang.

Little Baby. Pa rum pum pum pum
I am a poor boy too. Pa rum pum pum pum
I have no gift to bring. Pa rum pum pum pum
That's fit to give a King. Pa rum pum pum pum

As we trailed off Mattie sang the last line alone.

To lay before the king. Pa rum pum pum pum
On my drum.

When the song ended, we were all smiling; a family together on Christmas morning. There was no way to know if Nick would return, but I did know that I am a lucky man... who really loves Christmas.

BOOK TWO

SONGS *of* THE SEASONS

"There's a South pole," said Christopher Robin. "And I suspect there's a West Pole and an East Pole, though people don't like talking about them."

—The Complete Tales
of Winnie the Pooh
A.A. Milne

1

Auld Lang Syne

Nick didn't come back to the house on Christmas Day as I hoped he would. After the family finished our Christmas morning gift exchanges, I went out looking for him again, but I doubted I'd find him. Sure, he might have left early to retrieve his belongings, as Susan reasoned, but she hadn't been there when I invited him to live with us, or seen his face as he considered saying yes for one fleeting moment.

I don't know if he was too proud or too stubborn, but I had a feeling that, after I'd searched for him all through the holidays and finally shared one meal and a drink with him, we might never see Nick again.

At least I'd been able to pull him from the cold and say thank you, I reasoned. And Mattie had her gift from Santa.

Late Christmas afternoon, I was back at the house taking down lights in the front yard. David helped me for a while, then remembered something he had forgotten to do. He disappeared into the house, then came back with a couple of big envelopes.

"What's that?" I asked.

"Last two college applications," he said. "I didn't get them in the mail before Christmas but the mailman can pick them up tomorrow."

He showed me the big envelopes with computer-printed address labels and postage. The kid is organized. When he opened the mailbox to put them inside, he paused for a moment, then looked up at me.

"Did the mailman come yesterday?" he asked.

"No way; not on a Sunday and Christmas Eve. Why?"

"There's a letter."

"Someone probably dropped off a Christmas card."

"I don't think so," David said, as he pulled out a formal envelope and showed it to me.

It was from Harvard University Admissions, just as Nick had predicted.

THE NEXT THING WE KNEW IT WAS NEW YEAR'S EVE. Susan and I thought about going out for a champagne dinner to celebrate, but realized we'd just miss the kids and want to be home with them at midnight. So we had a New Year's Eve celebration at home like always, complete with black-eyed peas for good luck, cooked with Gramma Claire's recipe. If you don't like black-eyed peas at New Year's, then you're either not from Texas or there's something wrong with you. And even if you don't like them, you'll like Gramma Claire's recipe, which is about half bacon anyway.

When dinner was winding down, the conversation came back to Christmas and Nick.

"Mattie got a drum from Santa," said Molly, "and David got into Harvard. I'm beginning to wish I'd asked for something myself.

"Like what?" I asked.

"I don't know," Molly said. "You think Nick could reverse global warming? I mean his track record on the other stuff is pretty good."

"I don't think he actually got David accepted into Harvard," Susan said with pride. "David did that himself."

"Yeah. But how did Nick *know?*" David asked. "Dad, did he look in the mailbox when you guys arrived?"

"I don't think so. It was cold and we came straight from the car."

"Listen to yourselves!" Molly said suddenly. "If that letter had come next week, we'd say 'Nick was right; you did get in.' But the same day. On Christmas Day! It's like a miracle."

"Thanks a lot," David told her.

"Sorry," she said. "And I don't believe in miracles anyway. It's more like... what's the word?"

"Coincidence?" Susan offered.

"No."

"Psychic?" said David.

"No."

"Uncanny?" I said.

"Yeah. It's uncanny."

"What's uncanny mean?" asked Mattie.

"It means it can't be explained," Molly told her.

"Like my drum!" Mattie replied.

"What else did Nick say when you guys talked?" David asked.

"Yeah, where has he been all these years?" Molly wanted to know.

Suddenly I found myself being interrogated by my family about any and all things Nick. I filled them in with more details until Susan got to her main question.

"So... are you going back out to search for him?"

"I don't think so. He knows he's welcome here. But he strikes me as a guy who makes his own decisions."

Mattie had other concerns. "Papa, why doesn't he want to be Santa Nick anymore?"

"I don't know. It must be tiring being St. Nick. Maybe it's someone else's turn."

"So why did he sell us his home for so little money?" David asked

"And you said he sold his truck, too," added Molly.

"And gave his money away." Susan concluded. "He makes his own decisions, but I'm not sure they're good ones."

"They're not the decisions I'd make," I said, "but maybe those things didn't make him happy."

"So those are things he didn't want. But what does he want?" Molly asked.

"I don't know. Maybe he wanted to help other people, people like us, more than he wanted to own things. Maybe's he just looking for his place in the world. Maybe he wants to see a world where everyone does their part for others."

"That'd be something," Susan said. "It's New Year's Eve. Our resolutions for the coming year could be to help others."

Molly loved that idea. "That's cool, Mom."

"Then each of us should think about what we'd like to do this year."

"Not just think about it, Mom," Molly corrected her. "It takes more than thinking. It takes *doing.* Everybody thinks and talks but not many people do. The question is, what are we going to *do?*"

It was maybe five minutes before any of us spoke again. Coming up with an idea on what you want to do for others is harder than it sounds. I ran a dozen possibilities through my head—I'd met and seen so many people who needed help—but I couldn't quite land on what would make a difference or even what felt right. After a while, I looked up and saw that Susan was smiling.

"What?"

"Remember when my Mom got too old to leave her house? She wouldn't go to assisted living."

"Sure. She wanted to be in her own home."

"Which sounds wise, but she couldn't go to the grocery or cook."

"I remember," David said. "You went to the store for her. You cooked. You did everything."

"I did what I could, but not everything. But every day for three years, a volunteer from Meals on Wheels came to her door at noon—brought her lunch, checked to see if she was okay, and whether she needed anything. For three years."

"Which is why you donate to Meals on Wheels," I added.

"Exactly. I donate, but I don't *do.* I don't take meals to someone who needs help. I haven't become a reliable friend for anyone. I just write a check. So maybe I ought to see if they need me to start delivering meals."

"That's rad," Molly told her. "How are we supposed to follow that?"

"Molly, I don't think helping others is a competition."

"Maybe it should be. It'd be like reality TV!"

"I like all this," David said, "but I don't even know where to start."

"Start with the dishes," Susan told him. "I have a feeling you won't have many chances to wash dishes at Harvard."

We may put on a good Christmas light display and build a nice Solstice fire, but when it comes to New Year's Eve, we do like most American families—we turn on the TV and watch some pop acts we don't know, then we watch the ball drop at Times Square. This year, when we sang together at midnight, I thought it had never sounded more beautiful.

For auld lang syne, my dear,
for auld lang syne,
we'll take a cup of kindness yet,
for auld lang syne.

2

If Everyday was Christmas

I STUCK TO MY FIRST NEW YEAR'S RESOLUTION, which was to quit searching for Nick and start appreciating my life without guilt or regret. One day I drove past an old man with a white beard and didn't even stop to see if it was Nick, though I did take a quick glance in my rear view mirror.

We hadn't had another freeze since Christmas night, so my Valentine's Day present to Susan was to plant an early spring garden for her. I went to the Saturday farmer's market to look for seedlings, but the warm weather had caught the growers by surprise. I wasn't finding much to plant until I came to a guy who had the tailgate down on an old pickup and a truck bed filled with flats of tomato seedlings.

"Still might freeze," he told me in his South Texas accent. "If you plant now, be ready to cover them."

That's when I noticed the truck was candy apple red. I stepped back and got a better view—a vintage Ford pickup. My mind flashed back to the first time I saw Nick hammering that For Sale sign into his front yard, and the old red pickup parked in his driveway.

"Beautiful truck," I said to the farmer. "Mind if I ask where you got it?

"I don't mind," he said. "It's my favorite story."

He didn't even have to tell me, but it was good to hear the details anyway.

"A few years back," he said. "I was selling flowers and poinsettias from my family's farm at a Christmas market. An old guy with a white beard stopped to look at my poinsettias, and asked me if business was good."

"I told him it was slow and I needed a better way to display my plants; some way to get people to stop and look."

"So the guy showed me this truck; said he'd restored it himself. Did I want to buy it? There was no way I could afford a cherry truck like this. But he looked me over, got a funny look in his eye, and he said..."

"How much can you afford?" I blurted out.

The farmer looked at me in surprise. "How'd you know that?

"He sold me his house the same way. Have you seen him again?"

"I didn't see him for a long time. But a couple of years ago, I was making a delivery to a grocery store, and he was helping an old lady, loading bags into her car. After she left, he walked over and checked out the truck, said it looked like I was taking good care of her. Then he said he ought to get back to work."

"That's it?"

"No. By the next day, I was feeling bad about paying so little for the truck and seeing him in a minimum wage job. I went back to the store to catch his shift, but he wasn't there, so I asked the manager how I could contact him."

"And?"

"The manager told me Nick wasn't an employee; said he just came by and helped people out."

"Working for tips?"

"No, he didn't even accept tips; he just liked to help people."

I introduced myself to Jaime, the buyer of Nick's truck. We found a place to sit and I told him my story, including Nick's homelessness and nearly freezing to death on Christmas Eve.

"That's terrible," Jaime told me. "I should give the truck back to him."

"I don't think he wants the truck back any more than he wanted to move back into our house. I think he's got some idea about his life being some kind of an example, that he wants us all to make more effort to help other people."

"Man," Jaime said. "That sounds good, but how do I find the time and the money to do that? I still have to make a living for my family."

I told him I didn't know either, that I'd made the rounds to shelters and kitchens to do some volunteering, but hadn't felt like it was the right thing for me.

"Let me know if you come up with something,"

Jaime told me, "Maybe we can do something together."

When we got back to his truck, I asked where he got his seedlings.

"I grow them in South Texas. I've been working on farms with my parents and grandparents since I was a kid, and I can grow anything."

"Got any extras?" I asked, an idea stirring in my head.

Jaime was thinking, too. "We have thousands of seedlings planted, more than I can sell."

We started at Molly's school. She organized her middle school classmates to help and we planted a vegetable garden on the school grounds. We loved it and the kids loved it, and I knew I'd found something that felt right.

Jaime and I were planning to work a couple of hours a week planting gardens for a few schools or individuals, but word got out and one school turned into two, and two turned into twenty. We thought we'd plant gardens three or four hours a week, but three or four hours a day was barely enough. From February to June, we planted gardens at schools, at nursing homes, and in backyards. We planted vegetable gardens, butterfly gardens, memory gardens.

It was a lot of work—digging, weeding, mixing in compost, planting and mulching. After two weeks, I was so sore I could barely bend over. But after two months, I felt strong as an ox.

"Slow down," Jaime told me one day. "I'm getting tired just watching you."

But however hard I worked, Jaime worked harder. In April and May, we started looping back to what we'd planted and there were bushels and bushels of peas, cucumbers, beans, tomatoes, eggplants and peppers. Every garden was producing more than was being harvested, so we started taking the extra produce to a program called Angel House that serves breakfast and lunch to the hungry and homeless. Jasper had told me he'd eaten lunch there every Sunday for years. I'd volunteered there in January and didn't feel like I was helping much, but then I ended up feeding the same people anyway. Sometimes when I was digging hard, I'd find myself wishing Nick could see what he'd inspired Jaime and me to do.

By April we were picking more tomatoes than Angel House could use, so I asked Susan if Meals on Wheels would want them for the meals they serve. "We had three bushels of extra vegetables today," I told her."

"Three bushels," she said. "That's sweet, Honey, but I'm not sure that's enough to make a difference."

"Why? How many meals do they deliver?"

"Three thousand meals a day," she told me.

"Three thousand! Every day?"

"Yeah. Older people who are homebound, people with disabilities; more people who just can't get by on their own. There are a lot of people who need help."

Okay, so we were literally too small potatoes to boost the food supply at Meals on Wheels, but Jaime also knew people who needed help. His mother volunteered at Sacred Heart Cathedral's food pantry, distributing food to the needy of the Rio Grande Valley, including a lot of immigrants from Mexico and Central America. Once a week, Jaime drove the extra produce from Austin to McAllen and spent a couple of days working on his family's farm. When he drove back north, he brought more seedlings and compost.

One hot afternoon, we sat on the tailgate of Nick's truck and had a cold beer after we'd finished working.

"All our work," I asked Jaime, "you think it's doing some real good?"

"Sure," he told me.

"For them or for us?"

"What's the difference?" he asked.

Feliz Navidad

When we made our New Year's commitment, we hadn't considered how much time would be required or how they might interfere with family dinners. On top of my garden work and Susan's midday shifts at Meals on Wheels, David was tutoring several students on how to rock their SAT scores as he had, and Molly was teaching English to her classmate Sylvia Mateos, whose family had temporary residency after fleeing drug violence in El Salvador.

"I think I'm learning more Spanish than Sylvia is English," Molly told us one night at dinner.

Not to be outdone, Mattie had a weekend lemonade stand that did a booming business. Jaime was donating the lemons and honey from his family's farm, so Mattie's sales were all profit, with every dollar she raised going to Austin Pets Alive.

"Those dogs and cats are homeless, too," Mattie told us. "Just like Santa Nick."

I looked out the window one Saturday morning and saw something I'd never seen before. Mrs. Bumgarten outside her own yard, and she was talking to Mattie.

That looked like trouble, maybe a complaint about no sales or health permit, which Mattie definitely didn't have. I waited till the old lady was gone and went out to check on things.

"Everything okay?" I asked.

"Yes sir," Mattie said proudly as she showed me the five-dollar bill Mrs. Bumgarten had given her for a glass of lemonade.

I couldn't get used to Mattie calling me Sir. I liked it better when she said Papa, but we'd always encouraged our kids to say Sir and Ma'am to their elders. To my five-year-old daughter, I guess I looked old.

That evening at dinner, Mattie told us all about her conversation with Mrs. Bumgarten, who I suddenly realized wasn't nearly so mean and crazy as I'd thought. Mattie saying "Yes Ma'am" to Mrs. Bumgarten may have earned part of her five-dollar bounty, and now she wanted to know more about what she was suddenly calling, "customer relations."

Good manners towards adults had been the norm when Linda and I grew up under the gruff command of the Colonel. Please and thank you fell into the same category, and not as some holdover of Southern manners, but as a way to connect to people, and to be noticed for who you are.

"What else, Dad?" Mattie asked. "I want to connect with people so I can tell them why I sell lemonade."

"Just look them in the eye and talk to them. That's all it takes."

She looked at me suspiciously for a moment, looking me right in the eyes, then she said, "That's cool."

The thread of this family conversation lasted for several dinners. We talked about the importance of little things like opening doors as an everyday and ordinary kindness by any person for any other as a simple acknowledgement. Here we are, in this moment, you going your way and me going mine, probably hurrying, possibly lost in our own thoughts, then for one moment realizing that we're not in our day alone, we're in our day together.

We talked about how little effort it takes to offer a kind word, a pleasant greeting, or just a smile in passing; and how long those interactions resonate, echoing from one person to another to another and eventually back to you.

"When someone gives you a smile," Susan told us, "that may be your smile coming back to where it started."

Molly wanted us to remember the importance of speaking your mind, of speaking truth to power, and she reminded us that no voice was too small to not be heard, including hers.

"I don't think you're going to have any problem being heard," Susan told her.

Sometimes Mattie would look from one face to another and say, "Wait. I don't know what you're talking about," and we'd all stop and loop back to explain who someone was or what they'd said or done.

Sometimes we'd loop back too far and Mattie would say, "Stop. I know *that.*"

If these family stories sound like I'm making myself out to be some ideal dad, I'd like to point out that I am at best a work in progress, with Susan and the kids helping me to learn what being a good dad is. The more we share, the closer we become. I guess that's what a family is.

When one of the kids' friends joined us for dinner for the first time, you could see the transformation from 'what are you all talking about' to 'I have something to say as well.'

David's basketball buddy, Willie, stayed for dinner one night and we ended up talking about David's hero, Kareem Abdul Jabbar, and his journey from New York City public school hoops to UCLA to twenty seasons in the NBA as the greatest basketball player of his time. We also talked about his conversion to a man of Islam and peace, and a voice for truth in the world. This took a while because Mattie kept interrupting and saying, "Wait. How tall is he?"

The other details were fine, but somehow 7' 2" was too much to take in.

A few days later, I saw Willie's dad and for a moment I thought the Islam conversation had been too much for him.

"What did you do to my kid?" he wanted to know.

I stammered and said we were just talking.

"I know," he told me. "Now all he wants to do is talk."

"Is... that a problem?" I asked.

"I don't know half the stuff he wants to talk about! Turns out he's really into politics and social media stuff."

I didn't know what to say, and even though I didn't know what for, I finally said, "I'm sorry."

"Sorry?" he asked. "Why? I'm thanking you. If my kid wants to talk to me, that's a good thing, right?"

It was an odd conversation, and it made for a good story that evening at dinner. Now Willie's family was a little more connected and we were more connected to them. And I realized that meeting people, talking, smiling, were all a little like Nick's Christmas celebration where neighbors and strangers came together as a community.

I still like Christmas lights, but now I saw that the lights didn't bring us together. We just needed them to light up the world so we could see each other.

4

Pomp and Circumstance

MAY WAS A BIG MONTH FOR THE WALKER FAMILY. In one week, Mattie graduated from preschool. I thought the cap and gowns were a little over the top for kindergarten, but Mattie didn't, and that's what mattered. Then Molly graduated from middle school, not with a big ceremony, but with a field trip to tour Austin High, where she'd be replacing our graduating senior, who was ready to walk in his own cap and gown. I'd been sure David would be the Valedictorian of his class, but he had missed it by a fraction of a point, something that seemed of little consequence to him.

"Dad," he explained. "I'm already going to Harvard. And Mira is a better speaker anyway."

He was right about that, as Mira Patel's words to her fellow students and their parents rang loud and clear.

"Look at us! High school graduates!" she began, bringing a big cheer from her fellow students. "That's right. We have reason to celebrate. We feel like big shots now. Next we'll be college big shots.

Then we'll be big shots in the wider world, and the more important we become, the more we'll put ourselves first because that's what Big Shots do. But is that going to make us happy? Or make our families more proud of us?"

"Don't get me wrong. Every one of us should be proud of who we are and where we are going. Self-respect is a great strength; but self-importance is just a reflection of fear. Most of us are more afraid people will see we're a fraud, afraid we won't fit in, afraid we'll fail. You may think I'm not afraid of college because I made good grades in high school, but college scares me. I'm going to be away from my family for the first time, and that scares me a little, too. Fear is real. That's what we learned in history class when we studied Winston Churchill saying, "We have nothing to fear but fear itself."

"We don't face what the British people faced in World War II, but we do face an uncertain future. So I'd like to adjust Mr. Churchill's phrase a bit and say, we have nothing to live but life itself; and everything to love, including love itself."

"So don't be afraid to dream big. Have no fear of failure, which is the path to success, and never, ever be afraid to love."

When the ceremony was over and we were taking photos with David and his high school diploma, he nudged me and said, "I told you the right person was giving that speech."

JUST LIKE THAT, SUMMER WAS ON US. DAVID HAD been offered an early internship at Harvard, part of how he would be paying for that full ride, so we didn't have time for our annual fishing trip to New Mexico, and had to settle for a day-trip to the Hill Country.

The Christmas I met Nick, there was another "uncanny" Christmas present under the tree. My big brother David and I used to go fly-fishing with our grandfather in New Mexico, but after David died, that part of my life was over. I'd always wanted to have my own fly rod and often dropped hints about it to my parents and later to Susan, all to no avail.

A lot of Christmas mornings came and went without a fly rod under the tree. Then the year we bought Nick's house, hidden behind our tree on Christmas morning, there was a package with my name on it, but with nothing to reveal who'd given it to me. Just holding that split-cane fly rod felt life-changing for me.

The funny thing was, after all those years of waiting, I turned out to be a terrible fly-fisherman. Friends gave me lessons and I caught a few fish, but I didn't have the grace of a true fisherman like my grandfather Da Walker, any more than I had the grace of Gramma Claire at the piano. Each of us has to find our own way.

But David, oh wow, my son David took to that fly rod as if he'd been born to it. Whether we go to the Texas Hill Country or all the way to New Mexico, he seems guaranteed to catch fish. And that works out well because my favorite part of fishing turns out to be watching David fish.

Before his departure for Boston, we had a great day together at Guadalupe State Park in the Texas Hill Country. Wading quietly up into the current beneath the big cypress trees, David made beautiful casts and caught several nice Guadalupe Bass, while I stumbled along with my casting rod, far enough back that my splashing didn't scare his fish.

Watching him catch and release so many nice fish reminded me of something Jasper said one Sunday when I joined him for a meal at Angel House. I'd asked if he minded that most of these soup kitchens were run by churches and often started with a prayer, whether you wanted one or not.

"I don't mind." Jasper told me. "It's too late to catch me anyway. God already threw me back. But these preachers are all fishers of men. That's what Jesus said to the disciples. 'Follow me and I will make you a fisher of men.' I always liked that, but my favorite part is where Jesus feeds 5,000 people with five loaves and two fish. Now that was some righteous preaching, and I don't think anybody minded their dinner coming with a miracle."

Watching David catch fish after fish, I thought that he could feed the masses himself, it would just take more casts of that bamboo fly rod.

A few days later, David was gone away to college

and the beginning of the incredible life he was making. I was happy for him, but I was pained to see him go, and already thinking of Christmas.

I'll Be Home For Christmas

"I WANT TO GO TO HARVARD," MATTIE ANNOUNCED one evening over dessert.

"Then you'll have to study hard," I told her.

"No," she protested. "I want to go to Harvard *now* so I can see David."

I'd thought having two other kids in the house would lessen the emotional blow of our oldest going off to college, but that was not the case. Every evening at dinner, we all looked at his empty chair and we felt the hole in the conversation where David had often been the lead.

Thanksgiving and Christmas suddenly seemed very far away.

In addition to missing David, it was also hot; the hottest summer on record in Austin, like the summer before and the one before that, as Molly reminded us.

"Get used to it," she told us. "Every study shows that it's been getting hotter and will keep getting hotter. Then people are surprised when it does."

When I was in college, we didn't have

air-conditioning, which I find unthinkable now, though Molly often has us turning ours up or off, which is okay in an old house with high ceilings and good circulation. It's different if you're living on the street, hidden in a camp away from view and away from any cooling breezes, and I knew Nick and Jasper and several thousand more homeless people in Austin suffered in the hot Austin summers.

One upside to the weather was the booming business for Mattie's lemonade stand. She didn't like to hang onto the money she made, so either Susan or I drove her to the shelter every day or two to make her donation and visit the dogs, who all knew her and seemed to pin their hopes on going home with the little girl with the big smile.

But Mattie didn't want to adopt one dog, she wanted all of them to be adopted. Not long after her 6th birthday, she convinced the team at the shelter to allow her to bring one dog home every weekend. Every Saturday morning as she sold lemonade, Mattie's dog of the week would sit with her and an "Adopt Me" sign. And every Saturday morning, without fail, she sold all her lemonade and found a new home for a dog that really needed one.

The weather was too hot to plant gardens. For a few weeks, we went back to check on the earlier gardens, putting out mulch to preserve ground moisture, watering where we could and picking the ever-smaller crops of produce. The new norm was not turning out to be good for gardening. Finally we just gave up for the summer and Jaime decided to head home to South Texas for a while.

That meant I had a little extra time on my hands. One day I parked at the grocery store to do some shopping and I saw a mother with two kids struggling to push a cart full of groceries. She looked a little suspicious when I offered to help, but she didn't say no. Neither did the next person. Half an hour later, an older couple offered me a tip for loading their groceries.

"No, thanks," I told them. "But please give that to someone who needs it."

I told Susan about it that evening before bed, and she said, "I'll bet they did, too."

We strategized on ways to beat the heat, swimming in the cold water at Barton Springs and watching classic movies in the air-conditioning at the old Paramount Theater. I'm not sure why they chose to run a Christmas in July program, but I didn't miss the chance to take Molly and Mattie to see *Miracle on 34th Street*.

"So he *was* Kris Kringle," Mattie said later about Ed Gwynn's character who is nearly committed to an asylum for claiming to be the real Santa Claus, and who eventually works quite the Christmas miracle.

"Maybe he was," I told her, "but maybe he wasn't. I think it's up to the viewer to decide."

"Then he was," Mattie said confidently.

A month later, Mattie started elementary school and the traditional show-and-tell was the highlight of week one. Without mentioning it to Susan or me, she took the little origami Christmas tree and reindeer that Nick had made for her. When she told the students she'd met the real Santa Claus and that he'd made these presents, they all laughed and said she was stupid and that Santa wasn't real.

I was puzzled when Mattie's teacher called after school to tell us this story.

"Is Mattie in trouble because she believes in Santa?" I asked.

"Not at all," her teacher said. "I just thought it was incredible that she didn't back down."

Nothing quite so dramatic happened during Molly's first week of high school. She told us at dinner that she wasn't going to be popular at school but that she was going to be the President of the Student Council anyway.

"If everyone votes to elect the student council, but you're not popular, how do you get elected?" I asked.

"By being right," Molly told me. "These kids have a lot to learn."

David called every few days to tell us about something great at Harvard, which we loved to hear, but which I suspect left everyone feeling a little down, as his enthusiasm reminded us that he was going to be there for years.

One day I went looking for Jasper, who I hadn't

seen since our Sunday lunch. I drove around town for a while with no luck, then I remembered the metal scrap yard closes at 4 o'clock. I don't know why I didn't think of that earlier, but fifteen minutes later I was waiting when Jasper came pushing two carts down the street. He was moving them in a relay, pushing each cart twenty yards at a time, then looping back for the other one. That meant he walked 3 miles for every mile he moved the carts. And he looked about 30 miles worth of tired.

"Need a hand?" I asked.

"Two," he told me.

As he leaned on the handle of one cart, I retrieved the other one and pushed it up to the scale. After he sold his cans we drove to the same diner where I took Nick on Christmas Eve. The manager recognized me and even put us in the same booth.

We ordered some food, and I told Jasper I was worried about his being homeless, but he just laughed.

"I don't like to think of myself as homeless," he said. "Think of me as an urban adventurer."

We ate hamburgers and fries and fried okra, and drank a lot of ice tea. The restaurant serves beer and wine, but Jasper took a pass on that.

"Had to give it up," he said. "Caused me too many problems over the years. Maybe all my problems."

But now he had a problem that wasn't alcohol related. The guy who'd let him live for three years in his dilapidated garage couldn't afford the skyrocketing property taxes in his gentrifying neighborhood. After thirty years in the same house, the man might have to sell it.

With winter not far away, the timing of that sounded bad and left me lost in thought.

"I'm sorry," Jasper said into my silence. "It's not your problem."

"Maybe I'm making it my problem. Nick didn't want to live in my garage, but we could still fix it up for you. Not sleeping in a car. We could make it a garage apartment. Do you want to live on Wonderland Avenue? Not charity. You could take care of the yard in exchange for rent."

"That's the kindest offer I ever had," Jasper told me. "But I been down that street. Picked up cans there after you told me where you got all those cans you brought me. Saw your fancy house that your friend sold you. I don't belong on that street. I'm a trash man."

"You're a friend who needs a place to live. That's all that matters."

"Maybe," Jasper told me. "Maybe not."

6

100 Days of Christmas

WHILE I'M NO LONGER A CHRISTMAS CURMUDGEON, I still think the decorations, advertising and the music all start way too early. Writing a hit holiday song called *100 Days of Christmas* could be a real moneymaker. Just think how long they'd play it on the radio.

Before Nick came into our lives, my dread of the Christmas holiday usually started weeks in advance. I'd get infuriated by Christmas carols on the radio the day after Labor day, by Christmas displays that went up the day after Halloween, and by "last-minute" Christmas sales the day after Thanksgiving. I used to joke that on December 26, there should be a national campaign for only 364 shopping days till Christmas.

Since I met Nick, the commercialization bothers me less because I believe more in the non-commercial messages of Christmas, that Christmas truly is a symbol for the promise of peace on earth and goodwill to all.

This year my main issue was that I missed David. We thought he'd be coming home for Thanksgiving, but the flights were expensive. We were ready to spring for that, but he'd also met a girl who lived on the East Coast, and her parents had invited David for Thanksgiving.

"Are we losing him to that world?" I asked Susan.

"No," she reassured me. "Our bonds are forever. We just have to take full advantage of the time that we do get."

She was right, as usual. I knew he'd be home soon, and it would be great.

In early December as I laid out Christmas lights for a smaller display, a concession both to Molly and to my inability to put them all up without David's help, I wondered if I'd continue to put up fewer lights each year.

Looking at the smaller number of lights, my psychologist-counselor wife said I might be in partial remission from my OCD or Obsessive Christmas Disorder. Thousands of people across our country suffer from this malady, many of them sharing in group blogs about new lighting and sound systems, and taking pity on the slackers among us. Those who wait till the day after Thanksgiving are said to be dealing with their addiction by going 'cold turkey.'

I seem to be on more of a gradual withdrawal from my own addiction. Instead of three days to put up our usual display, the smaller one took just three hours. That evening when I threw the switch, Molly and Mattie went to the back to check the electric meter, which was barely humming along.

"Oh," Mattie said in disappointment.

"Shut the front door!" Molly said with glee. "We're no longer part of the problem."

David arrived three days later, looking three years older and three inches taller. That evening, he looked at the smaller light display and gave me his approval.

"I like it," he said, "and it'll be a lot easier to take down after Christmas."

No matter the size of the display, they still require tending. The next day, David was helping me replace a faulty string of lights when the mailman came up our sidewalk.

"You get the best Christmas cards," the mailman said as he handed me the bills and junk mail, and a handmade envelope with one-cent stamps going all the way around it, and a postmark from the North Pole. Suddenly I realized that I'd forgotten to ask Nick about the West Pole from the year before.

"Look," I told David," Nick must have sent me a reminder to go see Jerry the Peppermint Man."

But when I turned the envelope over, the return address was different. This one was from The East Pole.

With David helping refine my online search for a Nick connection to an East Pole, we quickly ruled out an upscale New York bar and restaurant called The East Pole and an East Pole coffee shop in Atlanta. But then we found a reference to a long-ago boast by a wonderful Austin writer named Edwin Shrake, who claimed to have discovered the location of the actual geographic East Pole. A man who loved a good joke, Shrake apparently never revealed the location of his discovery, but had long claimed you could actually take a bus there.

One search led to another, and the next thing I knew, I was taking an Austin Metro bus to the eastern-most stop on the city bus lines, headed to a community project called The Homestead, which I already knew was getting homeless people off the streets by building an entire neighborhood for them. Having met a lot of homeless people in the past year, many of them drunk, on drugs or generally disturbed, this sounded like an ambitious, worthy, and perhaps starry-eyed endeavor.

My visit wasn't unannounced. I'd called ahead and told my story to The Homestead's founder, Graham Neal, and asked if I could come there to look for Nick.

"The identity and whereabouts of those who live here is their own concern," Graham told me. "But you and anyone else interested in learning about our work are welcome to visit."

"Long ways to The Homestead," I called to the bus driver after it seemed like we had left most of Austin behind and already entered the countryside.

"It's the last stop on the line," the driver told me.

"Literally or figuratively?"

"Maybe both," answered a guy across from me who was wearing old army fatigues and a cap that said "Vietnam Veteran."

I didn't know what to expect at The Homestead, but I had a vague image of a large camp of homeless people: tents, shacks, maybe some power cords and water hoses snaking up and down to make it somewhat functional. There must be a good number of residents, I thought, for the bus had a several more passengers, men and women, young and old.

Finally the bus turned into a wide entrance past a sign that read "Welcome to the Homestead" and looped around a drive that circled a tall flagpole. From the door of the bus, I looked up to the top of the pole, half expecting to see some kind of East Pole flag flapping in the wind. Instead I smiled at the big Texas flag topped by a bigger Stars and Stripes.

"I never get tired of looking up at those flags," the veteran told me. "They always remind me that I really am home."

He pointed me towards the office where I found Graham Neal and a couple of his staffers all hard at work.

"You Michael?" Graham asked. Without waiting for an answer, he stood up and kept talking. "I'm about to make my rounds and deliver a couple of messages. Walk with me. Some people say it's good to see this place through my eyes."

From the offices, we moved to a general store that carried a surprisingly large number of staples, toiletries, fresh food and even had home-made tacos. It was clear that an enormous amount of planning, work and resources had gone into building this place.

"So, you told me your story," Alan said as we continued our tour. "Mind if I tell you mine?"

I was about to quote Jasper and say, "I got a feeling you're going to..." but Graham was already on his way.

"It's hard to know what life has in store for you," he said. "For twenty years, I was a minister and a family man. I thought my story was my wife, my kids, my church and my God. Then one day I discovered my story was actually the story of people who needed me. I'd been trying to feed homeless people, but had learned they needed more than food."

"What did they need?" I asked.

"It was obvious," Graham continued. "They needed homes; they needed family; they needed dignity."

While we walked, he showed me a community kitchen and a library, and a workshop with woodworking equipment and other tools that allowed the residents to develop skills and make a living.

"It took us ten years to build this place and to open up real homes to people who needed them; homes they take care of, homes they help pay for, homes in a community with caring instead of judgment."

"It's impressive," I told him.

He laughed. "First impressions are good ones. We have 300 people living here, all contributing in their own way, and every one of them is an individual who used to be homeless on the streets of Austin."

We came to the top of a hill where an outdoor dining area looked over the entire community.

"Where did the name come from?" I asked.

"Well, it's not 160 acres like Abraham Lincoln and Congress provided in the Homestead Act of 1862—for some people it's not much more than 160 square feet—but it's home, and as long as they pay some monthly rent and contribute to the general well being of the entire Homestead, that little piece of land and little house is theirs to keep. Just like the original Homestead Act, if they improve and care for their plot for five years, then it belongs to them."

"You must be proud," I told him.

"I am, but we still have a lot of work to do. We have entire blocks of empty spaces waiting for a tiny house to be built or for a quality trailer to slide in. The target here is a community for 600. If the City of Austin built three more Homesteads on the North, South and West sides, we could house every homeless adult in the city."

"What about people who don't want the homeless in their backyards?" I asked.

"The homeless are already in their front yards, and in front of their businesses, and on their street corners. We want to change all that. The alternatives are not good. What's the point of a great nation that throws 5 per cent of our population away like they were rotten tomatoes?"

Showing me the community's gardens and bee hives, Graham turned to me and said, "So what do you think?"

"I think I should have come here a long time ago."

I was convinced, but Graham had more to explain.

"People think homeless people are solely at fault for their situation, but homelessness is a story of poverty. There are many kinds of poverty: emotional poverty, medical poverty, poverty of family. That's the most common. A lot of the homeless don't have the people skills, the literacy and financial know-how, or even the emotional stability of those who achieve their piece of the American dream, but they are no less worthy in God's eyes or in mine. And every one of them, every single person who lives here, has talents that can still serve them and others."

"It's beautiful and it's humbling," I told him. "Can I ask you one more thing?"

"Anything, friend."

"Why do you think Nick sent me this letter and invited me to come out here?"

"I guess he wanted you to see his home," Graham said as he pointed at one of the small houses, a tiny cottage, white with blue trim windows and scrolled gingerbread trim on the eaves, and a bright red door.

I shook Graham's hand and thanked him. Then I stepped to the door and knocked softly.

"It's open," Nick answered. "Come on in."

7

It Came Upon a Midnight Clear

"HI MIKE," NICK SAID WARMLY. "I'VE BEEN expecting you."

We smiled and we shook hands, and then we exchanged a hug. It felt good.

"How do you like my new digs?"

I looked around the tidy cottage, a small front room with a kitchen adjacent and a doorway with a bedroom and bath.

"It's cozy."

"You mean little?" Nick said with a laugh.

"No, really, I like it. It's a lot nicer than we could have done in that garage."

"Mike, your offer was generous. But it wasn't what I was looking for."

"Which was?"

"A place where I was needed. This little house isn't my home. The whole neighborhood is. Which is why we're gonna sit on the porch."

Before we'd even sat down, a woman walking by lit up with a smile and said, "Hi Nick."

"Betty Jo," Nick replied, "How's your foot?"

"Better. I like that new doctor."

As she continued on, Nick hopped up quickly like he'd left something on the stove.

"Forgot the whiskey. I owe you a drink."

He came back in a jiff with two glasses and a bottle of bourbon.

"It's okay to drink here? There's no rules about that?"

"The rule is, if you don't cause problems and you contribute to the community, everything else is your business."

He poured us both a small drink, then said, "Wait, are you driving?"

"I took the bus."

"Perfect!"

Then he kept pouring. We had a lot to talk about. There was a chill in the air. We took a warming sip and both said, "aah."

More people passed by and every one of them waved to Nick. Several thanked him for some small thing he'd done for them.

"These are good people," Nick told me.

A long silence fell over us, then Nick spoke more softly.

"I told you about my wife, but not the whole story. There was a woman who loved Christmas. Sometimes I think she married me because my name was Nick or because of my birthday. Maybe both. We were young, and I didn't look anything like Santa Claus then, but destiny is a funny thing."

"I wish I'd met her."

"Yeah, you two would've gotten along just fine. Lemme tell you, she could bake some serious Christmas cookies. We didn't have kids, but every Christmas we invited families with kids into our home for a great meal, some good cheer, and a big plate of cookies. We had almost forty wonderful Christmases together, but one year I got a lump of coal in my stocking. Well, it wasn't coal, but it was still a lump. She found it on Christmas morning. How's that for irony? The doctors ran a lot of tests and told us it had already spread. Surgery was pointless and chemo not much better. They gave her a year. I didn't know doctors could be that accurate."

I looked at Nick, and could see that he was right there with her, all the way to the end, and even now.

"She didn't make the full year. Passed on Christmas Eve."

"Nick, I am so sorry."

"Thanks. That was a long time ago. Reminds me of how old I am."

"So you gave up on Christmas."

"At first. Nearly a year after she was gone, I looked into the mirror and realized I hadn't shaved since she passed. While I wasn't watching, I had finally become Saint Nick. To honor her properly, store-bought cookies weren't going to cut it. That was ten years before I met you. Ten years for the lights on my house to grow into a neighborhood celebration."

"You brought a lot of joy into peoples lives, Nick,

and I want to say thank you for me, for my family, and for thousands of others."

"I didn't do it for you, Michael. I did it for her. Everything I do, I do for my Marjorie."

"The house, the truck... the money, too?"

"Funny how much people move around these days. After ten years, there was hardly anyone left on Live Oak Lane that had known her, and every year I got more and more lonely in that big house. I already knew I didn't want to spend another Christmas there without her when I read one of those touching Season of Caring stories in the paper. It was about a single mom with two kids, too much cancer and no insurance. Money couldn't save my Marjorie, but my money could save that young Mom. Now every year at Christmas, those kids have a real live, loving mother, not a picture of one. You thought your house was my big gift to you, but the money you paid for that house changed that family's lives forever. That was the real gift."

"But why me?" I asked.

"I don't know; you came by at the right time; you took a leap of faith with me. Maybe I just had a sense that you were the one. Boy, was I right. You made that house a true home again."

"I'm just trying to follow the example you set."

"No, Mike. You're leading the way. You spent weeks searching for me when I was too proud to be found. You found me anyway and brought me in from the cold. When I was at the lowest possible point, you renewed my faith in all the things I'd once believed in."

"I hardly did anything."

"But you did a lot with little. I thought money was the way I could help people, and when my money was gone, I thought I was no more use to anyone. That's how I spiraled down. But on a cold night, for the price of a cup of coffee and some pancakes, you saved my life."

"I didn't even pay for them."

"Even better. That's when I realized I didn't need money to help others, I just needed love."

"Here's to love," I said, holding up my glass and toasting with Nick.

"To love!" he said.

ON THE RIDE BACK TO TOWN, THE SAME BUS DRIVER asked how I'd liked the end of the line.

"It's not the end," I told him. "It's the beginning."

"Just you and me riding back," he pointed out. "Mind if I turn up the Christmas music?"

"I'd like that," I told him.

I gazed out the window at the illuminated skyline of Austin as Willie Nelson began to sing *It Came Upon a Midnight Clear.* I sang along softly with the first couple of verses, then the song came to a third verse that I hadn't thought about since singing it in the church choir as a boy. Even then, it had been my favorite.

And ye, beneath life's crushing load,
Whose forms are bending low,
Who toil along the climbing way
With painful steps and slow,

As I listened to those words and Willie's wonderful voice, it felt as if the empty bus had filled with my family, as if my brother David, The Colonel and Claire, Susan and our kids, and so many more that I'd met on our street and on the streets of Austin were riding with me. And I could hear them all singing along with Willie.

Look now! For glad and golden hours
Come swiftly on the wing.
Oh, rest beside the weary road,
And hear the angels sing!

8

Little Drummer Girl

It was late when I got to the house, which meant I'd once again missed family dinner. I had a good reason, but David had only been home for a few days and he still hadn't told us much about the girl he'd met at Harvard.

When I came in the door, I heard David call from the dining room, "In here, Dad." And I found all my family waiting for me so they could serve dinner.

When Susan saw my face, she knew immediately. "You found him!"

I nodded and began telling them all about Nick and The Homestead. They asked more and better questions than I had. Finally I said that Nick or Graham could fill them in if we all went for a visit tomorrow.

"Tomorrow?" Mattie asked, her face a picture of concern.

"The play is tomorrow," Susan reminded me.

In my excitement, I'd forgotten the Christmas pageant at school that was built around the music of, what else, Little Drummer Boy. The day they announced this show, Mattie had come home in a mood of indignation.

"The teachers told me I couldn't play the part because the song was about a boy!"

"Oh no they did not!" Molly replied.

"Oh yes they did, too," said Mattie

"I'll fix that!" Molly told her.

"Wait," Susan asked. "Mattie, did you play the drum for them?"

"I did."

"And what did they say."

"They said we'd call it Little Drummer Girl."

So it was agreed. We'd all go visit the Homestead the day *after* tomorrow."

That didn't mean I wouldn't go sooner myself. The next morning I was back in Graham's office, grilling him on specifics about his community.

"Is there a waiting list to get in here?" I asked. "And do you have any empty homes available?"

"We have a couple of empty new homes, but the waiting list is long."

"How long?"

"Hundreds. Once we fund the next phase and find a couple of hundred donors, we can move most of those people in here."

"What about the trailer homes you showed me? They're nice, too. If I paid for one, could you move somebody into it right away?"

"Maybe. If we got the money quick enough, we

might be able to pull it off. But are you sure you want to buy a house?"

"I'm sure."

"Don't you think you should ask your wife first?"

"I bought one house without asking her, and that worked out okay."

"Sounds attractive, but no thank you," Graham told me.

"Why?"

"It's a lot of money. Talk to your wife; we're trying to bring families together, not break them apart."

IF YOU'VE NEVER BEEN TO A CHRISTMAS PAGEANT put on by first graders, you're really missing something. For starters, there were no first graders in the audience, just family members and my new friend Sam, the bus driver who said he'd be getting off work just in time to see it.

Every first-grader had some part in the show, starting with the three Wise Men, Joseph, Mary, the Innkeeper and his wife, and a chorus of angels. The rest of the kids portrayed sheep, camels, a donkey and the actual stars in the sky. And of course, there was the Little Drummer Girl, Mattie, who *really* played her Christmas drum.

Susan and I often have a small laugh at the expense of other parents who are overly proud of their perfect little child, so perhaps this was the night for the other parents to have that laugh right back at us.

For some reason, seeing that bull-headed, big-hearted little girl play that drum made me as proud as when David was accepted by Harvard. Drum or no drum, this girl was going places.

Near the end of the show, I glanced around to see if Sam had made it, and saw him at the back of the room, standing by Nick, who gave me a wink and a nod.

When the show was over, much to my surprise, Nick waited to talk to me.

"Great pageant," he said. "Marjorie would have loved that. So listen, I spoke with Graham about your idea, and he said to bring your friend out to have a look around. And he added one more thing."

"Talk to Susan?"

"Exactly. It's a big step."

"So what's the difference? When you offered to sell me your house, you told me I couldn't wait to talk to her."

"I was afraid she'd say no. This time, I know she'll say yes."

9

Christmastime is Here

UNLIKE THE YEAR BEFORE, THE WEATHER DIDN'T wait till Christmas Eve to turn cold. The whole week before Christmas it had been cold every night, and I'd thought about Jasper through much of those nights, wondering how he was, as I had with Nick the year before.

The next day I found him back in the park where we first met. He was pushing one cart half-full of cans, headed towards the scrap yard, and struggling to keep the cart moving.

To say he was happy to see me was an understatement, though he only let it show a little. I relieved him of pushing the cart, but he wasn't keeping up and I realized he needed the cart to lean on. He was worn out.

We made it to the scrap yard and he cashed out.

"Twenty dollars," he told me. "It's all this damn plastic. People don't throw out cans like they used to."

We drove a few blocks to a convenience store and I left the car and heater running when I went inside and bought us two cups of coffee.

"What's going on?" I asked as we sat in the car drinking bad coffee, which tasted good. "You seem tired."

"Oh yeah," he said. "I'm tired on top of tired. Have'nt been sleeping."

"Is your friend selling his house?"

"House is gone," he told me. "The garage and the car, too."

"He moved the whole house?"

"No, he got the new tax bill and sold the house a week later. I thought I had a little time, but the next day, the guy who bought it bulldozed it all."

"That's terrible. Where are you sleeping?

He shrugged.

"Remember my offer about our garage apartment?"

"Yes sir. I remember. But like I said, I don't belong in that neighborhood. Don't get me wrong. Your neighbors would probably be okay with it. It's not them; it's me."

"Okay. I've got another idea. Remember Nick?"

"How's he doing? I've been thinking about him and hoping he's okay."

"Nick is good. He's got a new home, and he offered to show it to you. It's a nice neighborhood; might even be some people there you know."

"Now?" Jasper asked.

"Is there a problem?"

"Look at me. I can't go to nobody's home looking like this. I haven't had on clean clothes for a week. My jacket's filthy and it stinks. This is no way to accept hospitality."

I looked him over, and he was right. His clothes looked bad, and he smelled a little ripe. It's amazing how much difference it makes to just have a dry place to sleep and even a hose to wash with.

So I picked up my phone and called Susan, who was waiting for me at the house.

"Can you bring my green jacket and meet me in half an hour?" I asked.

After I hung up, I took off the jacket I was wearing, and passed it to Jasper.

"Let's ditch yours," I told him. "I think this will fit you."

When we pulled into The Homestead and parked, the city bus pulled in behind us and Sam waved at me.

"Getting fancy in your own car, are you?"

I was a long ways from Live Oak Lane, but it still felt like home to see Susan and my kids getting off the bus. This time Nick was the tour guide, showing Jasper and my family the layout of The Homestead, introducing us to his neighbors as we walked along, exchanging Christmas greetings at every turn.

Winding through the little streets, we turned a corner and Nick pointed to his little cottage.

"This one's mine. This is my home."

"Cool!" said Mattie. "It's Santa's workshop!"

Funny I hadn't noticed it before, but with the

gingerbread trim and a wreath hanging on the red door, it did sort of look like Santa land. And I guess in a way, it was.

"You should be real proud," Jasper told Nick. "It's no small feat to get off the street and wind up in a beautiful place like that."

We were about to look inside when Graham caught up with us and introduced himself.

"If you don't mind," he said. "Let's walk a little further. I want to show you something."

Nick said he'd walked enough, and we should come back and see him when we were finished. So we walked on, my family and I following close behind Graham and Jasper as they talked.

"You got any family?" Graham asked.

"Yes, sir. Somewhere. I think my sister and her kids and grandkids are all still in Los Angeles. She loaned me some money when I was sick, but I still haven't paid it back."

"I bet she'd want to see you and hold onto you more than she'd want to hold that money in her hand."

"She's a good woman, but I can't go to Los Angeles. Even if I had a bus ticket, you gotta have an I.D. Can't renew a driver's license without an address, but I got nothing like that. I'm not anybody."

Graham gave a little laugh at that.

"What's so funny?" Jasper asked.

"You're about the fiftieth person who's said almost those exact words to me."

"And?"

"They all turned out to be wrong. You know the story about breaking the sticks? An old man summons his sons to offer his final words of advice and tells each of them to bring a stick. Then he ties all the sticks together in a bundle, which he hands to each son and says, 'break it.' None of them is strong enough to break the sticks, so the old man unties the bundle and hands each one stick, and again says, 'break it.' Now each of them easily breaks his stick."

"That's a good one," Jasper says.

"What makes us strong is everyone doing their part. Some people would laugh at the notion, but I believe I was called by God to do this work. Who knows, maybe you were called by God to come and see it."

"I don't know about that. I haven't been to church in a long time."

"Jasper, you probably know this as well as me. Lots of churches welcome the homeless, but not through the front door. When your clothes are bad and you look a little rough, you're more likely to be allowed in the back door for a cup of coffee and a sandwich and a prayer written on a little piece of paper. Here, the front door is always open, 24 hours a day."

"That's a good thing," Jasper said. "But I'm not sure any church is open to me. I spent a lot of long nights thinking about prayers that didn't work. He may strike me down, but I'm not sure I believe in

God any more."

"That doesn't matter," Graham said. "God believes in you. And so do all of us."

Having passed the last of the little houses, we came to a street lined with trailer homes, nice trailers that were built to be pulled around the country by vacationers and snow birds following the sun.

"These trailers are donated to us used," Graham explained, "but we redo them from top to bottom till they're just like new. They've got heat and air-conditioning, a bedroom, and a kitchen. All the comforts of home."

This may have all felt like a sales pitch to Jasper, who stopped and turned to Graham and my family.

"Listen, please. I like being with you people and I like this place, but I could never afford to live here. I have $40 in my pocket and I'm wearing Michael's jacket. Otherwise, I got nothing."

"You got friends," Graham said with a smile, "and that's a pretty good start. Walk a little farther with me. I see one that might be for sale."

As I looked ahead of us, it felt like I was peering into my own past, for there was an old man with a white beard, and he was hammering a For Sale sign into the yard in front of that trailer.

We walked up and Jasper stepped closer to Nick.

"I can't afford it," Jasper said. "I can't afford nothing. But I guess I should ask how much you want for it".

"Well," Nick said. "I think your friends have already

got that part figured out."

Unable to find any words, Jasper looked to me for some confirmation.

All I could do was nod my head, shake his hand, and say, "Welcome home."

10

Have Yourself a Merry Little Christmas

TWO DAYS LATER, ON CHRISTMAS EVE, THERE CAME a knocking on our door, a kind of a tapping or rapping, just a little like the clattering of tiny hooves. I started for the door, but Mattie got there first. She flung it open and said, "He came! He came! Santa Nick came on Christmas Eve!"

Nick gave her a hug, then he hugged me, too. And it still felt good.

David, Molly and Susan found us in the living room where Nick sat down on the sofa in front of the fire and once again let out a satisfied, "aah."

We were prepared and all had small Christmas gifts we'd wrapped carefully for Nick.

"Why don't you bring them by tomorrow?" Nick asked. "I'd like to give each one its proper attention."

"Whatever you like," I said. "I can bring your birthday present, too."

Nick laughed at that, and then he looked around at each member of my family as he laughed some more. He was clearly in a jolly mood.

He'd just come from Christmas Eve dinner with

his neighbors, including Jasper, who Nick said was already fast asleep in his bed.

"He wants to get an early start on his new job as the head of waste management for The Homestead."

"He starts work on Christmas Day?"

"It was his request. Said it's his first job in fifteen years and he's eager to get back to work."

Turning to Molly, Nick smiled, but didn't speak. Molly smiled back, then Nick lifted his eyebrows a bit.

"Well?" he finally said.

"Oh!" said Molly, as she jumped up and went to the other room where we soon heard the beautiful and just a little jazzy sounds of Silent Night coming from Nick's old Baldwin grand.

We listened for a bit, then Nick looked at Mattie with a smile. She smiled back, then he raised his eyebrows a bit, and Mattie figured it out.

"Oh right, time to go to bed."

"That's right. And speaking of sleep," Nick added. "It's getting late for me, too, but there's something I'd like to talk over with Mike."

While Molly switched to playing *Joy to the World,* Nick got another round of hugs and a couple of kisses too, which made his cheeks blush red. Wrapping up the song, Molly came back in to say her goodnight.

"I think maybe you really are Santa Claus," she told Nick, "because your piano is the greatest gift in the history of gifts. I love it so much."

"Well, keep practicing," Nick told her. "And keep

raising hell. That's what Jesus would be doing."

Susan and Molly both gave Nick a kiss and followed Mattie upstairs. That only left David, who'd been waiting for his own opportunity.

"What is it?" Nick asked.

"How did you know?" David asked. "How did you know I'd gotten into Harvard?"

"You really want to know," Nick said as he took David's hand and pulled him closer.

When David nodded yes, Nick said, "I saw it in your eyes. That and a lot more. How's that new girlfriend of yours? What's her name—Sarah, right?"

I couldn't remember if I'd told Nick Sarah's name, but either way, David looked surprised.

"You be good to her, son. I got a feeling you've caught a good one."

After David said goodnight, Nick and I were alone and he turned to me with a solemn look.

"What are you waiting for?" he asked. "Go get the whiskey. The good stuff like last year."

I was back from the kitchen in a flash and started to pour a drink for each of us.

"You're not driving, are you?" I asked.

Nick laughed again and I poured us both a double.

"Nick, can I ask you something?"

He smiled and said, "I got a feeling you're going to anyway."

"Last Christmas Eve, how did you come up with that drum you left for Mattie?"

Nick turned to look at me, tipping his head down and peering over his glasses.

"A drum?" he asked.

"Yeah. The red drum that Mattie asked Santa Nick for and that you left by the piano before you took off."

"Mike, I didn't leave a drum. But like I always say, theres a lot of St. Nicks in the world."

That's when it dawned on me.

"David. David gave her that drum."

"That'd be my guess," Nick said.

"But tonight," I added, "I see you're still out doing your part for the spirit of Christmas.

"Making my Christmas Eve rounds, you mean?"

"Are you?"

"What are you asking me, Mike? Do you want to know if I'm Santa?"

"Do you think you are?"

"Right back at you. Do you think I am?"

"I guess not, but there seem to be a lot of Christmas coincidences in your life: your birthday, your name, your wife Marjorie's love of Christmas."

"And you," he added. "So the boy who lost and found his love for Christmas wants to know if I'm St. Nick, Sandee Claus, Kris Kringle, The Emperor of the North Pole?"

"Well... yeah."

"Mike, how old were you when your big brother David told you there was no Santa—not a real one, anyway. Were you seven?"

"I think I was. So how did you know that?"

"Lucky guess. Listen, if there were a real Santa Claus, do you really think he could get a bunch of elves at the North Pole to make gifts for every kid in the world? No. When the legend of Santa began, maybe he was an old man who could whittle and his wife could sew, and they could give every kid in a village a gift. But imagine the pressure when the whole province starts talking about the mysterious Kris Kringle and his gifts. Or a whole kingdom. A continent. A world."

"Impossible."

"If there ever was a real Santa Claus, eventually he had to change his ways, and build a legend of giving. Eventually he had to make everyone Santa Claus."

"So you're saying..."

"I ain't St. Nick. You are."

"I'm not sure I follow you."

"Yes you do. There's no turning back, Mike. Ten years ago, you gave your injured son the heart and the will to live. And you gave your neighbors and all the other people who came down your street a belief in the joy of Christmas. You reminded them how much they love life and their fellow human beings, which is just about the hardest and most important thing to remember."

"Nick, I just put up the lights."

Now he took a long sip of his whiskey as he thought back to a more recent time.

"Lemme ask you. The next Christmas. When did you put up your lights?"

"A couple of weeks before Christmas."

"December 13. You counted back for the 12 Days of Christmas and turned on the first lights on December 13."

"You were watching?"

"How else would I know who's been naughty and who's been nice?"

"Now you're kidding me,"

"On Christmas Eve, when you and your son lit up that big Christmas tree out front, there were a thousand people singing *Joy to the World*. That's what I call giving by example. So the question is, who's Santa now?"

"You are."

Nick laughed, then he laughed some more and said, "Okay. Then we agree to disagree."

We'd finished our drinks and it was late, so Nick stood up to go. Standing at the door, we looked each other in the eye and shook hands, and I said, "Yes sir."

And he said, "Yes, sir, Michael, yes sir, indeed. I'm proud of you, son. And I'm guessing your father and your mother and your brother are real proud of you too. Merry Christmas, Mike."

I didn't think to ask if the bus was still running. I just watched him walk away, strolling right up the middle of Wonderland Avenue beneath the last few twinkling lights of Christmas. When he was gone, I shut the door and turned around to see Mattie sitting on the stairs. She had heard it all.

"He's *not* Santa?" she asked in a small voice.

"Sure he is," I said as I picked her up. "He's just not the only one."

I was about to carry her up to bed when we heard something on the street, a sound that seemed both strange and familiar.

"What's that?" Mattie asked. "Did he come back?"

Running to the door, we flung it open, and there in the middle of Wonderland Avenue, directly in front of our house, was a reindeer.

This was no origami paper reindeer. And it wasn't a lighted, Christmas display reindeer. This was a real, live reindeer, with tall antlers and steam coming from his nostrils and mouth when his breath met the cool air.

Suspecting I'd had too much whiskey with Nick, I looked to Mattie, who was pointing with a look of wonder.

"He remembered," she said softly.

Afraid to say another word, we just looked on quietly. Then after a few long moments, the reindeer shook his head up-and-down as if he heard someone calling him, then he ran up the street in the direction where Nick had gone a few minutes earlier.

Stunned and speechless, Mattie and I leaned our heads forward and turned them in unison as we watched the reindeer disappear into the darkness.

We stood there in the cold a long while to see if there would be more reindeer, or maybe a Santa calling to them in the night, and finally Mattie turned to me with an important question.

"Do we tell mom?"

I thought about it for a moment, considering the likely reaction from Susan.

"No way," I said. "That was only for you and me."

Stepping forward, Mattie turned in the direction where Nick and the reindeer had disappeared, Then her voice rang out into the night.

"Merry Christmas!" she called out. "Merry Christmas!"

The End.

A CHRISTMAS SONG

Postscript

FROM SEA TO SHINING SEA, THERE ARE AN estimated ten million men, women and children living on the streets and in the temporary shelters of America. They are grandmothers and grandfathers, mothers and fathers, sisters and brothers. And they are children. It is impossible that each of them is responsible for their situation. We are all in this world, together, and one mark of a great nation is how its people unite for the good of all. I am confident that in our great nation, we need to and can do better.

I'd like to extend a hand of thanks to Alan Graham, the founder of Community First Village in Austin, Texas, for his work and his words of wisdom and love. Likewise to his staff and supporters, and to all who are committed to doing better for our brothers and sisters in need.

A wise man named Willie Nelson once told me, "You can always trust in love."

I believe him, deep in my heart, and hope that you do, too.

www.ingramcontent.com/pod-product-compliance
Lightning Source LLC
Chambersburg PA
CBHW060538310726
48982CB00009B/1297/J

* 9 7 8 1 8 8 1 4 8 4 1 2 7 *